ADVANCE PRAISE

"*Odsburg* is a novel of wild mystery told with high wit and serious heart. It's full of the surreal weirdness of actual human existence. Tompkins delivers big fun with insights delicate and strange."

—Michael Bible, *Empire of Light*

"Welcome to *Odsburg*: a clever mess of pamphlets, menus, ingredient lists, overheard fragments, diaries, and stories that exist only in the mind of Matt Tompkins—a collection of ephemera that somehow adds up to a delightful, funny, endlessly entertaining work of fiction."

—Amber Sparks, *The Unfinished World and Other Stories*

ODSBURG

Matt Tompkins

OOLIGAN PRESS • PORTLAND, OREGON

Odsburg
© 2019 Matt Tompkins

ISBN13: 978-1-947845-08-4

Ooligan Press
Portland State University
Post Office Box 751, Portland, Oregon 97207
503.725.9748
ooligan@ooliganpress.pdx.edu
www.ooliganpress.pdx.edu

Library of Congress Cataloging-in-Publication Data
Names: Tompkins, Matt, author.
Title: Odsburg / by Matt Tompkins.
Description: Portland, Oregon : Ooligan Press, 2019.
Identifiers: LCCN 2019005600 | ISBN 9781947845084 (pbk.)
Classification: LCC PS3620.O58135 O37 2019 | DDC 813/.6—dc23
LC record available at https://lccn.loc.gov/2019005600

Cover design by Jenny Kimura and Hanna Ziegler
Interior design by Des Hewson
Paper texture used with permission from vecteezy.com

Printed in the United States of America

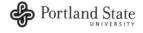

FOR KORI AND GRETA

ODSBURG

A SOCIO-ANTHROPO-LINGUI-LORE-OLOGICAL STUDY

By Wallace Jenkins-Ross

DEDICATION

Above all, I should note that this book owes its existence—its raw material and its reason for being—to the good people of Odsburg, Washington. They welcomed me into their town, in some cases even into their homes, and, at the very least, they did not chase me out or press charges against me for trespassing or loitering or invasion of privacy as I gathered the various documents included in this book. So, to the people of Odsburg: Thank you. While I may have assembled it, this book is yours.

AN INTRODUCTORY NOTE
ABOUT MYSELF AND MY METHODS

It is my privilege, Dear Reader, to introduce myself and to share a few details about my work.

My name is Wallace Jenkins-Ross, and I am a socio-anthropo-lingui-lore-ologist. If you've never heard of such a thing, you are not alone: I'm the only one I know of. This is because socio-anthropo-lingui-lore-ology is a hybrid discipline that I devised during my time as an undergraduate, the constituent threads of which I trust you can suss out from the name. Sadly, the field has not gained much traction outside of my own studies, a failing that I can only attribute to a powerful academic hegemony and steadfast adherence to the status quo.

When I tell people my title, they almost always ask me what a socio-anthropo-lingui-lore-ologist does. And I tell them, though the title is complicated, what I do is simple: I collect stories. Stories from ordinary, everyday people, just like you. By extension, I also collect publications, artifacts, and ephemera that tell stories. If I were writing a mission statement, it would say that my discipline is the preservation and elevation of local lore, personal histories, and primary documents, with an emphasis on otherwise overlooked marginalia.

I practice an embedded participant-observer method of immersion in the subject culture. The goal is to be invisible in plain sight—to achieve total integration by living as the locals do. In the case of Odsburg, it meant I spent most of my time wearing soft flannel shirts, worn blue jeans, and hiking boots, all exceedingly comfortable, albeit quite different from my tweedy academic norm. I retained my accustomed glasses and beard, as they seemed immaterial to my choice of "uniform," and because they feel as much a part of my face as do my nose and mouth.

Immersion also meant that I spent a fair amount of time drinking draft beer, eating pub food and diner fare, and sipping copious quantities of strong coffee. This was also a departure from my usual macrobiotic whole-food regimen, but again, not an unwelcome one. I should say, for a complete outsider, I found that from the beginning of my time in Odsburg, I felt very much at home.

It bears mentioning that my methods have been called unorthodox—even "impertinent" and "unprofessional"—by some in the academic intelligentsia. Rest assured, I am undeterred by such criticism and remain dedicated to my craft. However, the unavoidable upshot is that my research is unaffiliated with any educational institution, and thus 100 percent independent and self-funded.

Lest you get the wrong impression, I am not a man of endless means. About ten years ago I received a substantial insurance payment upon my parents' untimely death in a train derailment. To make something good of a bad situation and honor the memory of my unfortunate forebears, I felt the best way to spend it (or to have spent it, as it is now all but gone, the barrel-bottom balance supplemented with odd-job earnings) was to invest that grief-laden windfall in furthering the field of socio-anthropo-lingui-lore-ology.

And so I have.

AN ADDITIONAL NOTE ABOUT ODSBURG AND MY EXPERIENCE THERE

A bit of background seems in order. For this, I refer you to the following, copied with permission from the website of the Odsburg Tourism Bureau:

> The Town of Odsburg was founded by brothers Josiah and Jeremiah Ods in 1854 on the northern bank of the Sillagumquit River. It sits in the heart of scenic Trumbull County in western Washington State, nestled in the green, bucolic realms south of Seattle and north of Portland, Oregon, with the majestic Cascades gazing down from the east and the mighty Pacific abiding to the west.
>
> At its inception, the town was little more than an encampment—a stopping point for merchants making their way along trade routes between cities, fisheries, and mining towns up and down the coast.
>
> In the 1870s, after the arrival of the railroad, the hamlet flourished as a spiritualist destination when it became home to a faith healer named Alva Moonstone. A contingent of her devotees can still be found today, sometimes making pilgrimage to her grave on the outskirts of town.
>
> Odsburg became a modest industrial hub in the late nineteenth and early twentieth centuries. In

addition to a cannery and a lumber mill, the area saw a variety of light industrial production. Doorknobs, milk bottles, and cutlery stamped "Proudly made in Odsburg, WA" can still be found in thrift and antique shops throughout Washington, Oregon, and into Northern California. However, with one exception (OdsWellMore Pharmaceuticals, which perseveres), manufacturing interests have gone from the area.

The town is also currently home to Odsburg College, a small, well-respected liberal arts school founded in 1904 by a philanthropically inclined industrialist before he and his fellows packed up and left.

In 1996, Odsburg was voted "Fifth-Quaintest Town in America" in a poll in *Small Towns & Villages* magazine. In 2001, it was voted one of six Silverhair Meccas by *Retire Well* magazine. The town boasts a bustling array of pubs, restaurants, coffee shops, and other small businesses, as well as charming bed and breakfasts, and offers easy access to both the natural and metropolitan attractions of the greater Pacific Northwest.

But the true charms and singular quirks of Odsburg cannot be conveyed by statistics and accolades such as these. Come see for yourself: Experience Odsburg.

Now, one would be forgiven for asking, of all the places in the world, why I would choose Odsburg as the subject of my study when surely there must be hundreds of towns much like it. My friends and family certainly asked. However, I'm afraid you may be as unsatisfied with my answer as they were. I can only say I felt an incontrovertible pull in its direction. Once the name had entered my mind (I encountered it on one of the aforementioned milk bottles while rummaging for a writing desk in the jumbled bargain basement of a Sausalito antique shop), I found that I could think of little else. I felt I had no choice but to go there, to immerse myself and to document the place and its populace.

And so I did.

I decamped to Washington abruptly, having only recently returned home to Northern California from a stint in the high desert of New Mexico, before which I had been several years in New England and upstate New York. My files contain copious notes from each of those places, but alas—I've been told—nothing publishable. Nevertheless, I am wed to my work, which means I must keep traveling and collecting, and which is why I find myself here, at the far end of my thirties, divorced, driven to drift, with next to nothing to my name, save for this little book before you and a few hodgepodge belongings.

But I digress.

I lived (on a shoestring) and worked (nonstop) as a participant-observer in Odsburg for approximately two years. During that time, I came to know and admire the place and its people as I compiled this humble yet—I hope—literarily, ethnographically, anthropologically, folklorically, and psycho-spiritually significant volume. Perhaps that's a lot of pressure to place on what is sure to be viewed as a minor work, but I feel the need to justify, if only to myself, the opportunity costs of the production.

What follows is a diverse collection of local legends, notes and letters, historical records, community announcements, advertisements, and other miscellany, as well as numerous orally recounted personal stories, some told to me directly, and others that I overheard while sitting in cafes, pubs, and parks. I have transcribed the personal stories from field audio recordings (I carried a compact digital audio recorder everywhere

I went in Odsburg), and I made every attempt to transcribe them verbatim, aside from some lengthy pauses, preambles, throat-clearings, and tics and fillers such as "um" and "like," which I largely redacted for readability. A handful of the stories I observed transpiring and have retold in my own words.

The documents are not presented in chronological order, but I have grouped or paired some, where pertinent, by commonality of theme or subject matter. In the explanatory notes preceding each piece, I have specified the source and nature of the document and provided a bit of added context.

Now: I will not keep you any longer from the stories that, when all is said and done, are the heart of the matter.

Welcome, Dear Reader, to Odsburg!

A LIST OF THE DOCUMENTS
CONTAINED HEREIN, WITH
TITLES ASSIGNED BY ME FOR
REFERENCE AND EXPEDIENCY

TOWN FOUNDERS

Below is an excerpt from the original Odsburg town char-
ter, c. 1854, on file in the archives of the Odsburg Historical
Society, which occupies a modest, cozy office suite on the
second floor of the building that houses the Odsburg Public
Library—a stately, red-brick box with concrete columns
located on historic Front Street.

The town historian, Francine Glasbury, was generally help-
ful, though she seemed perplexed as to why I wished to copy
down this particular section of the charter to the exclusion of
others. She also seemed confused, albeit in a kind and polite
way, by my general presence and purpose in the town.

I should mention that I learned, only after arriving in the
town, that Odsburg and its inhabitants are prone to atypically
high rates of abnormal behavior and extraordinary phenom-
ena. Theories abound among the locals concerning the reasons
for this proclivity. Some attribute it to the town being built on
an ancient and powerful "psycho-spiritual energy vortex" (this
is the commonly used and generally agreed-upon terminology
among believers of this theory). Whatever the true cause of
such phenomena may be, the document below suggests that
the trend dates back a long time—to the town's official incor-
poration, at least.

Unfortunately, I was unable to ascertain the precise location
of the below-mentioned Trumbull's Corner, but I suspect it to

be somewhere in the vicinity of what is now the town square, along which runs Main Street and around which are clustered many of the town's businesses, including the Thirsty Dachshund Pub, Stardust Coffee Bar, Anderson's Tavern, and the Goose & Gander Grill.

Section XXIV: Trumbull's Corner

BE IT specified herein, with regards to that area of the Town of Odsburg called and known as Trumbull's Corner, defined and delineated as by the boundaries of Glover's Meadow to the North, Weare's Brook to the South, Hume's Field to the East, and Greene's Fir Stand to the West, that in these environs, so-called supernatural, occult, unusual or, at the least, atypical occurrences and happenings have been witnessed and attested to, at various times and by various Town residents.

THEREFORE, let all Town residents be so informed, for their own good and for the good of all others, and be advised to approach the aforesaid location with all due caution and, if and insofar as it be at all reasonably practicable, to avoid attending upon said place altogether.

FURTHERMORE, let all Town residents be advised that if they are to attend upon Trumbull's Corner, they shall be wise to avoid bringing children, horses, and dogs, as these are known to be most sensitive to such energies, emanations, and happenings as have been known to occur at said place.

SEEKING ADVICE AND/OR
ASSISTANCE RE: MOUNTAIN LIONS

What follows is a personal story transcribed from a field record-ing. The speaker was an addled-looking man in his mid-thirties with matted hair, dark circles under his eyes, and several days' chin stubble, whom I met riding the #9 Trumbull County Transit bus to GroceryPlus Supermarket. He did not give his name, although I asked for it repeatedly. He seemed distracted, fretting constantly with the frayed cuff of his sweatshirt sleeve and tap-ping the toes of his sneakers erratically on the rubberized floor.

This also seems an opportune place to mention, regarding the various theories behind the town's peculiarities, that there are those, perhaps more practical-minded, who by way of explana-tion cite Odsburg's proximity to a state-run psychiatric hospital a few miles away in the town of Klester. I cannot say that I favor one explanation over another—the supernatural and the psycho-logical have always struck me as branches of the same tree—nor am I suggesting that the gentleman who gave the account below was a psychiatric patient. On the contrary, he seemed like a rational, levelheaded person in what I would describe, at risk of understatement, as a challenging situation.

There's a family of mountain lions living in my basement.

I say "family" because I know there's more than one, but I don't know exactly how many. If I knew how many, I would just give you the hard number. Like "there are five mountain lions living in my basement." But that's only a guess.

To be fair, "a family of mountain lions" may not be accurate, either. I'm not sure they're related. To be really precise, then, there is a *group* of mountain lions living in my basement. And in case you're wondering, there's no proper term for a group of mountain lions. I looked it up.

Not a herd, or a pack, or a gaggle, or a pride—not even a murder, as it is with crows, which I think would be apt.

Please notice that I haven't entirely lost my sense of humor yet.

Anyway, apparently, they—mountain lions—typically fly solo. Solitary beasts. So no one ever bothered to name a group. What I want to know, then, is how I managed to get so lucky. A whole group of them in *my* basement!

I'm being facetious, if you couldn't tell.

I want to note here that I did plan to have my house custom-built. It's a beautiful house, by the way. Three beds, two baths, open floor plan, in a desirable neighborhood. I did a lot of research. Figured out all the details. Took out a sizable loan from the credit union to finance it. It's a thirty-year mortgage, but worth it. At least, that's what I kept telling myself.

I thought I'd planned for everything, but I did not plan to have mountain lions living in my basement. So I suppose that goes to show you can't plan for everything. That is what I call a *lesson for life*.

During construction, I stopped by every week to see how it was progressing. One day, I noticed the foundation was open, exposed to the elements, while the construction crew framed and walled the main structure of the house. It occurred to me that if it rained, water would get into the foundation. I said something to the construction workers, but the foreman said not to worry, they had it all under control. Then he waved me off like a buzzing fly. Told me to relax, leave it to the experts.

But do you know what did not occur to me when I saw the gaping foundation? That a group of mountain lions might nest in the basement. So I didn't say anything about that. My mistake, I suppose.

I think they must have come down from the hills north of town. The mountain lions, that is. Not the construction crew. The construction crew came in from Graysville. I didn't even know the hills had mountain lions living in them.

But I guess they do—or, rather, they did.

So anyway, wherever the mountain lions came from, now they're in my basement. Let me restate for the record: the possibility of this happening did not occur to me. It simply did not occur. Apparently, it didn't occur to the construction foreman either. Or to any construction foreman, ever. Or to the people who wrote the building codes. There's nothing on the books about it at all. So, for these reasons, the foreman insists he's not liable. He says he followed standard procedure and this is my problem alone. He also said they had everything under control. I guess that's just an expression.

Still, whoever may or may not be liable, there are mountain lions in my basement. And I'll tell you something else: I didn't even know they were there. Not at first. I know that sounds silly. How could anyone overlook a group of mountain lions? Well, I'll tell you how. It was early spring when we moved into the house, and the mountain lions must have been sleeping very deeply. You'll notice that I didn't say "hibernating." That was intentional. According to my research, mountain lions don't hibernate.

Call it what you will, then. Napping. Snoozing. Lying in wait. Whatever. They were down there in the basement, quiet and still—presumably way back in the crawlspace, because how else did we miss them?—for at least a couple of weeks. And then, as soon as the weather started to warm, the mountain lions awoke.

They must've been hungry by then, because they started scratching at the basement door. I remember thinking, *What could that be?* I peeked through the narrow gap underneath the door in the kitchen and I saw big tan paws and sharp claws and fangs and fur and whiskers and several large, pink noses. When I put all this together, I had my answer.

Mountain lions.

They were scratching from the inside-the-basement side, where they were. I could hear them from the other side, the outside-of-the-basement side, where I was. So at least we were on opposite sides of the door, the mountain lions and me. I guess that's what you call a *silver lining*.

They were also snuffling, which was quieter than the scratching, but still audible. It made me feel weird to think that they were smelling me. And when I say *weird*, I suppose I really mean *terrified*.

I called the Department of Fish and Game and asked if they could help me. Maybe bring over a couple of those neck snare things, like you see on those nature-man shows. Pull the lions out, take them back to their native habitat, let them loose. They said it's not their problem either. Those guys and the construction foreman, two of a kind.

They also said this particular type of mountain lion is endangered, meaning it's illegal to kill them. It would even be a felony if I let them die of neglect in my basement.

So then I thought maybe, if they're so rare, I could make a few bucks off them. Sell them to a zoo. Nope. Selling them is a criminal offense, too. Endangered animal trafficking.

When I tried to go to sleep that night, I could still hear them scratching from my bedroom on the second floor. My wife and our baby son were both scared. My wife was scared of the idea of being mauled by mountain lions. My baby son was just scared of the unfamiliar scratching sound. He is too young to know what mauling is, or what mountain lions are. Another silver lining.

I went to the garage and got a saw, which I used to cut a narrow slot in the basement door. The slot is for sliding raw steaks into. The raw steaks are for feeding the mountain lions. The feeding is so they would hopefully calm down and stop scratching.

After all, that door wouldn't stand up to all that scratching forever. I mean, sure, it's solid wood—really high-end construction—but come on: those multiple sets of four-inch claws, working day and night? Piles of rich blond wood shavings had begun to collect and grow larger on the threshold. And the math behind it so brutally simple: the bigger the piles, the thinner the door.

Where was I? Oh, the feeding slot. The feeding slot seemed like the only sensible thing to do. And the steaks appear to appease them. There's a lot less scratching now. But at what cost? I mean, I can tell you at what cost. I have the receipts. Steaks are not cheap. So it's not a sustainable solution. Not to mention, at risk of stating the obvious, the mountain lions are still there. And the scratching and snuffling haven't stopped, they've just lessened. So I can't say the problem is solved. De-escalated, I guess. With an endless and very expensive series of raw meat Band-Aids.

And to top it off, word has gotten out to the animal rights people. A whole bunch of them are picketing out front. They're carrying signs with slogans:

ANIMAL RIGHTS: NO ANIMAL WRONGED.
PROTECT THE LIONS' PRIDE.

At first, I thought they might be of some help. Raise awareness, get these animals back to the wild, where they belong. But no; their position is exactly the opposite. The mountain lions have chosen to live in my basement. They should be allowed to remain. We've taken over their habitat, so this is payback. The activists insist they'll *intervene immediately* if I try anything that might harm the lions. Or anything that might infringe upon the lions' *inalienable rights*. Which apparently includes living in my basement.

So no help there, either.

And did I mention the thing about the laundry? The washer and dryer are in the basement. So we can't do laundry, considering the mountain lions. I know—we could go to a laundromat. But we spent two grand on a new washer and dryer. And now I'm going to go and spend even more money to wash my clothes at a laundromat? In their inferior washing machines smelling of chlorinated mold? With their harsh powder detergents that digest delicate fabrics? In their nonadjustable, overheating dryers that will burn my merino sweaters to charred husks of lint? That will shrink and contort my Egyptian cotton shirts into expensive, nappy rags? And then what will I wear to work, when all my clothes are ruined? I'm a professional—an engineer, for Pete's sake. I have an advanced degree. I work at OdsWellMore. I can't just go to work in a, a pair of greasy sweatpants. So, no. No, thank you. I will not throw my wardrobe away in those ill-maintained lint traps! Those churning boxes of imminent fire hazard! Damn it all to hell!

Wait, stop.

Deep breath.

I think I'm misplacing my anger about the mountain lions and taking it out on the idea of laundromats. I'm not angry at laundromats. Not really. Laundromats don't deserve that kind of badmouthing. They're perfectly productive businesses that provide a needed service to society. I just lost my head for a minute. Please excuse that outburst.

Anyway. If you have any idea what to do about the mountain lions, please let me know. I'm kind of at the end of my rope, here. Damned if I do, and all that. A felony to kill them, a felony to sell them, and a danger to keep them around. I mentioned I have a baby, right? And a wife? They can't defend themselves against a mountain lion—much less against an unknown number of hungry, captivity-crazed mountain lions. And that door won't hold forever. I may have to take matters into my own hands, consequences be damned.

But not right now. Not yet. I don't want to do anything too rash, too hasty. Not until I've exhausted all my other options.

So, like I said: if you have any ideas, I'm open to suggestions.

For now, though, I'm headed to the GroceryPlus. We're all out of steaks.

A WORD FROM OUR SPONSOR

What follows is a transcription of a radio advertisement from OdsWellMore. The ad played frequently on WODS 89.3 FM— Odsburg's home for all your smooth-listening favorites of yesterday and today.

I acquired the recording by holding my digital audio recorder up to a dust-covered, ceiling-mounted stereo speaker at the Thirsty Dachshund. I reached the speaker by an acrobatic feat, deftly balancing atop a wooden table on my tiptoes—and all for your benefit, Dear Reader! From that perch, by the large plate-glass front window, I stood eye-to-eye with the eponymous wiener dog painted on the shingled sign outside. Up close, I could see that the dog's eye, which from a distance appeared as a solid black dot, was in fact a tight, winding spiral.

It is worth noting that when played back slowly for transcription purposes, the voice of the speaker, which sounds positively cheery at normal speed, instead sounds ominous—I might even go so far as to say "villainous." Don't ask what happened when I played it backward.

Although the company has a significant role in the town's economy, some locals suggest (largely under their breath) that the town's high concentration of extranormal occurrences might in fact have something to do with OdsWellMore—specifically with regard to dubious disposal practices for pharmaceutical compounds, and the possibility that these compounds may be entering the groundwater.

Introducing Odsphoriq, a new offering from your friends at OdsWellMore, a trusted name in pharmaceutical life-enhancement products and a pillar of Odsburg's local economy!

In clinical studies, Odsphoriq has been shown to increase feelings of well-being, calm, peace, ease, joie de vivre, sans souci, and generalized happiness in a plurality of users. If you, or someone you know, suffer from depression, sadness, boredom, displeasure, ennui, sangfroid, angst, or any other form of chronic non-bliss, Odsphoriq may be able to help. Ask your doctor if Odsphoriq may be right for you.

Odsphoriq is a mood-altering psychopharmacological compound, the underlying operating mechanisms of which doctors have no real knowledge or understanding.

Odsphoriq has been shown to cause side effects in a percentage of individuals who use it. Side effects may include dizziness, dry mouth, coughing, loss of appetite, gain of appetite, stabilizing of appetite, weight gain, weight loss, and breathless impatience.

Cold feet, hot head, fever, chest pain, insomnia, hives, boils, anxiety, derangement, skin irritation, eczema, dandruff, alopecia, French twists, loss of humility, appetite for danger, reckless impulsivity, purple hair, ingrown toenails, outgrown fingernails, froggishness, flu, and congestion have also been shown to occur.

A small number of patients have reported experiencing obsessive compulsions, compulsive obsessions, hemophilia, hemophobia, heartburn, carpenter ant infestation, recalcitrance, money grubbing, royal flushes, neck burn, rug burn, uncomfortable fellatio, destitution, noblesse oblige, Napoleon syndrome, overwhelming guilt, or irrational disbelief.

Taking Odsphoriq may also put you at increased risk of debilitating envy, quivering of the extremities, unusual hubris, nerve damage, fleas, flights of fancy, phantom limb, loose bowels, tingly feelings, numbness of the ankles, gingivitis, rampant fear, oxidation, reactivity, mood swings, mood jumps, mood spins, pinky-finger calluses, food cravings associated with pregnancy, pregnancy, underdeveloped ego, waxing philosophical, hair loss, hirsuteness, and uncontrollable itching.

If you are taking Odsphoriq, consult your doctor immediately if you experience gigantism, elephantiasis, shrunken testicles, blue blood, pie in the eye, cataracts, jaundice, germaphobia, German measles, kaleidoscopic vision, ham shanks, halitosis, hematuria, vertigo, visions of grandeur, the grumps, audiovisual hallucination, identity crises, crises of faith, Earth crises, slouching, memory loss, bursitis, grunge, lack of empathy, nagging doubt, or sudden death.

Most side effects are mild to moderate and subside within one to five years of discontinuing use of Odsphoriq.

Ask your doctor for a free sample if you think Odsphoriq might be right for you!

MEL AND THE MICROPHONES

The following was spoken by Mrs. Karen Hines, eighty-two, of River View Drive. I recorded Mrs. Hines's story when I delivered a pizza to her home. As I mentioned, I am not above picking up an odd job to stretch my dwindling funds. While in Odsburg, this included delivery driving for Crustella's Pizza.

I initially concealed the audio recorder inside my thermal pizza carrier, but Mrs. Hines, after hearing the recorder beep conspicuously, assured me she didn't mind being on the record, and said it was good just to have someone to talk to.

Karen's husband, Mel, could be heard inside the house, and his voice can also be heard in the field audio recording as a continuous and barely audible background murmur, commentating on the pizza transaction and other events, some in real time, some remembered. For dramatic effect, select quotations from Mel are interspersed throughout the following text.

Microphones. Microphones. Microphones.

In the kitchen, microphones. In the bathroom, microphones. In the bedroom, microphones. In the garage and the office and the den and the great room; in the laundry room, the breakfast nook, the dining room; in the foyer and the mudroom and the guest bedroom; in the backyard, the front yard, the side yard, and the driveway; in the car and the half-bath and the patio. Microphones.

None of them are live. None of them plugged in. None of them even have cords running out of them. None with batteries. No little glowing green lights. No functioning microphones whatsoever. Some of them aren't even really microphones. Some of the microphones are just tea strainers— the kind with the silvery metal mesh ball on the end of a stick—stuck into an empty toilet paper tube and wrapped with duct tape. They only look like a microphone if you squint. Or have bad eyesight. Or if you aren't looking too closely. Some of the microphones are toys or pictures printed on plain white copy paper. Microphones and fake microphones and images of microphones. All over. All over the house.

My husband, Mel, has advanced dementia. He's eighty-five years old. Used to be a sportscaster; a play-by-play announcer. His whole career. Forty-plus years. Highly respected, widely known.

And then there's me, the devoted wife. Married five decades, our four children all grown with kids of their own. Busy living in far-off cities. And me, still here haunting this old, echoing Victorian. Me, with nothing to do but watch and wait and wonder, remembering everything. My mind still clear, still sharp.

But Mel, he forgets.

I got the idea to set up the microphones when I noticed him one afternoon, talking a mile a minute into one of my hairbrushes. That's how this all got started.

"And the chicken is cooking, browning, sizzling! Folks, this is going to be a dinner for the ages!

Oh my, that's the buzzer. Stick a fork in it. It. Is. Done!"

Before the microphones, Mel wouldn't say two words all day. But with a mic—or something that looks *similar* to a mic—he'll talk day in, day out. 'Til he's hoarse. 'Til I turn off the lights and go to bed. And sometimes he'll keep right on after that. I don't mind, even when it keeps me up nights. Play-by-play, though it's not conversation exactly, is better than nothing. It's better than silence.

Most importantly, it makes me feel like my husband is still here. Like he's still my husband. Anyway, more so than I felt during the long, staring, dribbling hours before.

"They're on the couch, watching television!

They've finished two programs, and I think they might go for three!

What a night, folks. What. A. Night!"

Phil Fleming was Mel's commentating partner. They worked together, side-by-side, for thirty-two years. A long, successful marriage in its own right. Phil's dead now, has been for more than a decade. When Mel gets going, he often speaks to Phil. It makes me sad, because it breaks the illusion that my husband is truly lucid—the impression that he's really talking to me. But then, so does the fact that he's commentating on all of life's little occurrences as if they were major sporting events. As if they warranted this type of ticker tape narration.

Narration that reminds me of the grandkids' constant, chirpy self-commentary on their social media apps, their mobile devices. The kind of chatter that says, *I'm here, I'm here, I'm here.* The kind that reassures the speaker that she's alive. If only because she can hear herself talking.

As if all the little moments—all the tiny details of your life—deserved attention, and documentation, and broadcast.

"This is it folks, the moment we've all been waiting for!

She's putting on rouge!

She's spraying on the Aqua Net!

She's taking out her rollers!

It's all coming down to this, folks!

And she could be—is she?—yes, she's ready for a night on the town!"

OENOPHILIA

The following is a reprint. The original document was handwritten—in a tight, scratchy script that got wobblier as it went—on a piece of marbled, faux-vellum stationery paper.

I obtained this document when it was hurled at me in the form of a crumpled, soggy ball from the window of a passing car—I think it was a late-model Honda Civic—as I trudged through February slush from the Thirsty Dachshund—or maybe it was Anderson's Tavern?—to the Silver Spoon Diner for pancakes—or was it Crustella's for a slice?—at 2 a.m. on a Saturday.

Ophelia's Wine Bar, I later learned, was a dimly lit lounge tucked down a short flight of stairs at the back of the Goose & Gander Grill, behind the Golden Beak banquet room— something of a matryoshka doll (or, if you prefer, turducken) of food and drink establishments.

Ophelia's Wine Bar

Patron Name:___Pete Glenacre___

ID Checked:___X___.

Sampling Menu: Deluxe Wine Flight

Tasting Notes:

1. Citrus / Plum / Fresh berries
2. Oak / Butter
3. Honey / Lavender / Sage
4. Caramel / Vanilla / Clove
5. Ginger zest / Juniper / Rosemary
6. Anise / Fennel
7. Night air / Tobacco smoke / Spearmint gum
8. Slurredwords / Jennifer / Matchbook
9. Sweatsalt / Lipstick
10. Tongue tip
11. Jennifer'sboyfriend'sfist / Mouthblood
12. Toothfragment / Barpolish / Naugahyde
13. Lackbalance / Shoeleather / Floortile
14. Copperpenny / Stomachacid / Nothing

THE WATER CYCLE

The following was transcribed from a field recording. The speaker is Eric Hawkins, thirty-three, a deputy in the Trumbull County Sheriff's Office, who shared his story with me over pints at Anderson's Tavern. At times, Deputy Hawkins appeared to grip the metal seat of his barstool, as if for fear he might float away. He periodically glanced outside, and when he did, the whites of his eyes reflected the liquid blue-green of neon beer signs in the window.

I will throw in one further possibility here (as good here as anywhere, I think) as to Odsburg's high level of inexplicable happenings: it may have something to do with the supernormal gloom and the damp and fickle weather patterns in this corner of the Northwest—whether by direct barometric effect, or indirectly as the dreary climate inclines the locals to all manner of self-medication. Admittedly, this theory (of my own devising) would not explain why Odsburg is so affected, while other locales in the region are comparatively unscathed. The validity or veracity of this theory is wholly unconfirmed, as is the case, if I am being candid, with all the others put forth. In the end, I suppose it is up to each of us to decide what to believe—an increasingly difficult feat, it would seem, given the proliferation of messages, myths and (mis)information by which we are constantly bombarded.

Deputy Hawkins, for what it's worth, is several years younger than me and has two children in Odsburg Elementary School. This made me wonder about the path not taken, about the singular journey of parenthood. Fraught as it is, and ill-suited as I consider myself for the role (suffice it to say, we all have parents, and childhoods, and with that comes certain uncheckable baggage), I wonder if I will have missed out on something important.

When I was twelve years old, my dad evaporated. He'd been sitting in his ratty recliner reading the newspaper. I was across the living room, cross-legged on our old corduroy couch. I looked up from my *Fantastic Four* and he was—how do I put it?—he was somehow even less present, less *there*, than usual.

To be fair, my dad was always kind of airy. Perpetually distracted. Prone to daydream. But this was different.

It started with his thinning, bark-brown hair—the same hair that I inherited. It grew wispier still as it wafted away. This evaporative process continued until his plaid sweater-vest, pleated khakis, and socks were empty. They all just deflated, laid out flat on the still-reclined lounger. His newspaper slumped like a crumpled pup tent over top.

A moment later, he regrouped—re-formed as a fog in the air above his chair. Then, slowly but steadily, he drifted downward and disappeared, sucked into the belly of the dehumidifier that ran year-round to keep the house from molding.

Late that afternoon, my mom came home. Despite my loud and tearful protests, she pulled the bucket from the dehumidifier. She walked it, sloshing, out to the garage and dumped it unceremoniously down the utility sink.

And so my dad became a fully integrated part of the Odsburg Municipal Sanitary Water System. I had learned all about this from Mrs. Wilkins in science class. My father would now be undergoing filtration, chlorination, and fluoridation. Then he would be pumped into a reservoir—from whence he could flow to who-knows-where within the county—to be drank, bathed in, used for washing clothes or cars or dishes, or even to fill a toilet. In any case, he'd be washed back into one drain or another, to repeat the process all over again.

Of course, there was another possibility: That he would escape. That he would break free of the open circuit that is the municipal water system. That he would become instead a part of the greater water cycle—the one Mother Nature put into motion billions of years ago. We had learned about this, too, in science class.

He could run out of a garden hose and into the ground; evaporate from a wash basin or water glass near an open window; wind up in a dog dish and be escorted outside as a trail of slobber; be splashed from a kiddie pool or a water balloon; the list goes on—and on and on.

Eventually, by one means or another, my dad did make it out. I know because he came back to see me.

The first time, he was a wave on the Sillagumquit River. I was sitting on the bank, tossing rocks, watching them splash and listening to the plunks and plonks. He rolled right toward me and broke a few feet away. I knew it was him because it was exactly his corny dad sense of humor, to wave to me as a wave. I could almost hear his voice: *Look, Eric—I'm waving!* My mom was nearby on a bench reading a book, but I didn't bother to call to her. She gave me the strangest looks and talked about doctors any time I mentioned my dad.

The next time, he was a cloud. I couldn't think of how to say hi to him or how to let him know I saw him. He was so high up and I was all the way down on the ground. I got so sad I started crying, which turned out to be pretty perfect, actually. My tears evaporated and rose up to join him in the sky. Then I think neither of us felt quite as lonely or as sad.

The last time was just a few weeks ago. He must've found his way back into the city water system, because he turned up in my coffee. I think this might have been his idea of a practical joke. Once I spotted him, I couldn't bring myself to drink the coffee. Not that I think he would've particularly minded, but it was just a little too weird. I mean, it's one thing to slap a puddle high-five; it's another thing entirely to cannibalize your father. So instead I ate the rest of my breakfast and left him sitting there in the mug. When I was done eating, I told him a little bit about my week. The wife and kids were already gone, to work and to school. It was nice to sit and spend some time together—just the two of us.

Sometimes I wonder if I should be angrier at him for disappearing. People have suggested it often enough—my mom, my friends, my therapist. But somehow I don't blame him—or, rather, I don't see the use in holding a grudge. He probably lost as much as I did when he went away, maybe more. And anyway, how much choice did he have—how much say in what happened? Maybe we're just slaves to our nature. Maybe I shouldn't make excuses for him, though. Maybe it's just easier to tell myself he didn't *choose* to leave us.

Before long, I had to go to work. On my way out the door, I poured my dad into the flowerbed so he'd be free to go about his business. I know he'll find his way back when he can. And who'd want to be stuck inside a coffee mug all day?

If it ever comes to it—and let's face it, maybe someday it will—I hope my kids will have the decency to do the same for me.

ABOUT THE NEIGHBORS

The following is a reprint of a publicly distributed, independently (and, I might add, crudely) printed circular. The original document is a multi-page pamphlet, evidently copied on a machine in ill repair. I found a copy tacked to a "community announcements" bulletin board at the Odsburg Public Library. I also saw several copies stapled to telephone poles around town.

I retyped the document so as to spare you the needless taxation of reading the streaky, smudgy, toner-heavy original. All-caps typography has been retained to preserve the sense of shouting, which seemed to me an integral feature of the artifact.

CITIZENS OF ODSBURG!!!! DO YOU THINK YOU KNOW YOUR FELLOW CITIZENS OF ODSBURG???? YOUR FELLOW ODSBURGERS??? THINK AGAIN!!! YOU DON'T KNOW THEIR LIVES, THEIR DREAMS, THEIR HOPES AND FEARS, THEIR SORROWS, THEIR EXPERIENCES!!! HERE ARE SOME THINGS YOU DIDN'T KNOW ABOUT YOUR OWN NEIGHBORS!!!! JUDGE NOT LEST YE BE JUDGED!!!!!!!

1. YOU PROBABLY ALREADY KNOW THAT ROGER AND FRANCINE GLASBURY HAVE SEVEN (7) MINIATURE FRENCH POODLES. FRANCINE DRESSES THE DOGS IN TINY SWEATERS AND PEACOATS AND GROOMS THEIR FUR INTO BOBS, MOHAWKS, MULLETS, AND AFROS. PEOPLE SNICKER AND MAKE SNIDE COMMENTS WHEN THEY PASS ON THE STREET. THE GLASBURYS DON'T TELL ANYONE THIS, BUT THEY HAVE SEVEN POODLES BECAUSE THEY WERE ABLE TO HAVE ZERO (0) KIDS. TRIED FOR YEARS: NO LUCK. IVF, HORMONE THERAPY—YOU NAME IT, THEY TRIED IT. IN CONCLUSION, THEIR POODLES ARE THEIR CHILDREN. NOW DON'T YOU FEEL BAD ABOUT SNEERING AND JOKING? DON'T YOU??????? ??

2. ART MONK, 64, LONGTIME ODSBURG POST OFFICE EMPLOYEE, RANKED IN THE 99TH PERCENTILE ON THE MENSA INTELLIGENCE TEST AT AGE 22 AND IS A CERTIFIED GENIUS. HE CREATES AND SOLVES COMPLEX LOGIC PUZZLES IN HIS SPARE TIME, WHICH HE SHOWS ONLY TO HIS CAT PERCIVAL. ART NEVER WENT TO COLLEGE AND BARELY FINISHED HIGH SCHOOL, BUT HE ACHIEVED THE HIGHEST SCORE IN THE HISTORY OF THE CIVIL SERVICE EXAM, WHICH IS HOW HE LANDED HIS MAIL-CARRIER POSITION. HE WILL RETIRE NEXT YEAR AFTER 34 PRODUCTIVE YEARS OF SERVICE. HE AND HIS PARTNER, TOWN COUNCILMAN BILL DAVIS, HAVE PLANS TO MOVE TO A COTTAGE ON THE OREGON COAST. JUST GOES TO SHOW, YOU CAN'T JUDGE A MAN BY HIS COVER, WHICH IS TO SAY HIS UNIFORM, OR STATION IN LIFE, OR MAYBE WHAT I MEAN TO SAY IS, THERE'S NOTHING AT ALL SHAMEFUL ABOUT BEING A MAIL CARRIER!!!!!!!!!!

3. JESSILYNN POTACK, 8, A MEMBER OF MISS DECKER'S THIRD-GRADE CLASS AT ODSBURG ELEMENTARY SCHOOL, HAS A PROSTHETIC LEFT LEG FROM THE KNEE DOWN. WHEN SHE WAS 5, THE LOWER PART OF THE LEG SPONTANEOUSLY TURNED MAGENTA AND FELL OFF. ALTHOUGH THERE WAS NO KNOWN CAUSE, JESSI'S FATHER, JAMES POTACK, BLAMES HIMSELF. HE BELIEVES HIS HOT AND UNPREDICTABLE TEMPER AND FREQUENT ANGRY OUTBURSTS CAUSED THE LIMB (ALONG WITH WHAT HE BELIEVES TO BE THE CORRESPONDING PIECE OF JESSI'S SOUL) TO

WITHER AND DIE. ALTHOUGH HE GOES TO THE
METHODIST CHURCH ON SUNDAYS, JAMES'S TRUE
RELIGION IS A DEEP AND COMPLEX COLLECTION
OF BELIEFS ABOUT EMOTION AND ENERGY THAT
HE HAS CONCOCTED FOR HIMSELF AND SHARED
WITH NO ONE ELSE (DON'T ASK ME HOW I KNOW).
NONE OF JESSI'S CLASSMATES ARE AWARE OF HER
PROSTHESIS, NOR IS HER TEACHER, BECAUSE SHE
WEARS LONG PANTS OR DRESSES AND STOCKINGS
EVERY DAY, EVEN IN THE SUMMER. WHEN ASKED
ABOUT HER MODE OF DRESS, SHE SAYS, "MY FAMILY
IS VERY CONSERVATIVE." YOU NEVER KNOW WHAT
SECRET OBSTACLES AND STUMBLING BLOCKS,
WHAT PERSONAL DEMONS, ANOTHER PERSON
MIGHT BE GRAPPLING WITH, DO YOU? NO, YOU
DON'T!!!!!!!!!!!!!!!!

4. TOWN COUNCIL CHAIR MARTIN LONGACRE, 53, IS
CURSED AND DOESN'T KNOW IT. ON A TRIP TO THE
FLORIDA KEYS SEVERAL YEARS AGO, HE ANGERED
AN INFLUENTIAL PELICAN, WHICH MARKED
HIM WITH A SECRET SIGN DETECTABLE ONLY
TO OTHER BIRDS, AND TO A FEW DISCERNING
PEOPLE, MYSELF INCLUDED, WHO KNOW WHAT
THEY'RE LOOKING FOR. NOW ALL THE MOURNING
DOVES, ROBINS, STARLINGS, AND CORMORANTS IN
ODSBURG POOP CONSTANTLY ON MARTIN'S CAR
AND HOME. HE DOESN'T BOTHER WASHING THEM
ANYMORE BECAUSE THEY WOULD BE COVERED
AGAIN IN MINUTES. HE SCRAPES ENOUGH OFF THE
WINDOWS TO SEE OUT AND TRIES TO GO ABOUT
HIS BUSINESS AS BEST HE CAN. I'M TEMPTED TO

MAKE A JOKE HERE ABOUT SOMETHING BEING FOR THE BIRDS, BUT I WON'T BECAUSE THIS IS SERIOUS, NOT OPEN MIC NIGHT AT THE CHUCKLE HUT, AM I RIGHT?????????????????????????

5. ELLA ROBINSON, 76, WAS BORN WITHOUT A BELLY BUTTON. ALTHOUGH SHE WAS BORN IN THE USUAL WAY, AND HER FATHER SWORE HE REMEMBERED CUTTING THE UMBILICAL CORD, HER ABDOMEN IS INEXPLICABLY SMOOTH AND UNMARKED. AS A RESULT, ELLA'S MOTHER, LIDIA ROBINSON, SUSPECTED ELLA WAS AN ALIEN PLANTED TO GATHER INFORMATION ABOUT THE HUMAN RACE, PERHAPS TO BE USED AGAINST US IN A FUTURE INTERGALACTIC CONFLICT. BECAUSE OF THIS, LIDIA WAS ALWAYS A BIT COLD AND RETICENT WITH ELLA AND, TO ELLA'S DISAPPOINTMENT, EVEN REFUSED TO SHARE HER SECRET AND MUCH-ADMIRED COFFEE CAKE RECIPE, WHICH ELLA HAS BEEN UNABLE TO RECREATE BUT INSISTS WAS THE BEST SHE EVER HAD!!!!!!!!!!!!!!!!!!

6. KARATECHOP HIRSCH, 48, OF RIDGE ROAD (WHOSE PARENTS LET HIM NAME HIMSELF ON HIS THIRD BIRTHDAY), IS PETITIONING THE TOWN COUNCIL TO LET HIM MARRY A 40-LB. BAG OF DOG FOOD. WHAT YOU DON'T KNOW IS THAT THE DOG FOOD PETITION IS A PLOY. KARATECHOP'S TRUE DESIRE IS TO BE JOINED IN CIVIL UNION WITH HIS PERSONAL ROBOTIC HOME HEALTH AIDE, ISSUED TO HIM BY THE ODSWELLMORE EXPERIMENTAL TECHNOLOGIES DIVISION UNDER

THE PROVISIONAL NAME E-NUM-O-R8, AND WHICH KARATECHOP HAS RENAMED SAUNDRA. THE STRATEGY: FIRST ASK FOR SOMETHING ABSURD, THEN BARGAIN DOWN TO WHAT YOU REALLY WANT. KARATECHOP MIGHT NOT BE AS CRAZY AS HE SEEMS. HE IS, HOWEVER, BARKING UP THE WRONG TREE, BECAUSE THE TOWN COUNCIL HAS NO JURISDICTION OVER MARRIAGE LICENSES OR CIVIL UNIONS. WHAT KARATECHOP HAS IN STRATEGIC CUNNING, HE LACKS IN BUREAUCRATIC KNOWHOW!!

7. CARMICHAEL JONES, 35, OF ODSBURG GARDENS APARTMENTS, LIVES WITH HIS WIFE CARMICHELLE AND THEIR CHILDREN CARMACK, CARMONGO, AND CARMAPOLIS. EVERYONE THINKS THEY NAMED THEIR CHILDREN OUT OF A SENSE OF OVERWEENING VANITY. IN REALITY, THE KIDS WERE SO NAMED BECAUSE CARMICHAEL LOST A CHILDHOOD BET WITH HIS BROTHER DEAN. DEAN BET THAT CARMICHAEL WOULD FALL IN LOVE WITH AND MARRY CARMICHELLE, WHO LIVED DOWN THE STREET. HE INSISTED IT WOULD HAPPEN, AND LAUGHED LONG AND HARD ABOUT IT. CARMICHAEL SAID HE WOULD NEVER FALL IN LOVE WITH AND MARRY THAT GIRL, OR ANY GIRL. IN FAIRNESS, CARMICHAEL WAS 8 AT THE TIME, AND DEAN HAD THE ADVANTAGE OF BEING FOUR YEARS OLDER, WITH THE INSIGHT OF AGE. THE BET DICTATED THAT, IF THE TWO MARRIED, ALL THEIR CHILDREN WOULD BE NAMED "CARM-SOMETHING" WITH THE ENDINGS TO BE CHOSEN

BY DEAN. IF THEY DID NOT MARRY, DEAN WOULD HAVE TO NAME ALL HIS CHILDREN "BUTTFACE," FOLLOWED BY A NUMBER CORRESPONDING TO THE ORDER IN WHICH THEY WERE BORN. IN THE END, CARMICHAEL AND CARMICHELLE WERE TOO PERFECT FOR ONE ANOTHER TO WORRY ABOUT SILLY NAMES. CARMICHAEL TOLD CARMICHELLE ABOUT THE BET ON THEIR FIRST DATE, AND WHEN SHE FELL DOWN LAUGHING, HE KNEW SHE WAS THE ONE. DEAN NAMED HIS KIDS BUTTFACE 1 AND BUTTFACE 2 ANYWAY, PARTLY OUT OF BROTHERLY SOLIDARITY AND PARTLY BECAUSE THAT'S JUST HIS BRAND OF HUMOR. BUT THEY GO BY RUDY AND MARLISE!!!!!!!!!!!!!!!!!!!!!!!!!!!

MY FELLOW CITIZENS!!! LOOK NOT AWAY AND HEED MY WARNING!!! DO YOU THINK YOU KNOW WHAT LIES IN THE SECRET HEARTS AND MINDS OF MEN AND WOMEN??!! DO YOU THINK YOU CAN JUDGE YOUR NEIGHBOR, YOUR FELLOW MAN, YOUR FELLOW WOMAN????? YOU DO NOT KNOW!!! JUDGE NOT LEST YE BE JUDGED!!!!!!!!!!!!!!!!!!!!!!!!!!!

PUT ON A HAPPY FACE

What follows is transcribed from a field recording. The speaker was a harried-looking middle-aged woman with frizzed, bleached-blond hair. She wore a brown velour pantsuit and green cat-eye glasses. I overheard her speaking to a second middle-aged woman while they were standing in line at Stardust, a locally owned café that has had some trademark trouble with a certain multinational coffee corporation. I had secreted my digital recorder behind a pastry box, so the speaker had no reason to suspect she was being recorded. I never caught her name.

"Botox," I said.

"What?" Derrick said.

"Botox," I said. "And collagen."

I'd already spoken with Dr. Mund, over at Odsburg Family Practice. He'd agreed to write the scripts. Administer the injections, too. All to help me teach Danny a lesson. Mort—he insisted I call him Mort—was very agreeable about the whole idea. Truth be told, I think he might have a little thing for me. Not too surprising. I may be forty-two, but I've got pleasing curves in the proper places, and I've been told I have a seductive way of speaking.

When I told Derrick, though, he shook his head.

"No way," he said. "Isn't it dangerous? What is it, even?"

My husband is such a weenie.

"Botox is a neurotoxin," I said. "Which means it blocks nerve signals. And collagen—collagen comes from bones. It's completely safe."

I thought that would shut him up, but no.

"I don't think so," he said.

Derrick has no vision, no … theatrical flair. This was my umpteenth plan for a "teachable moment" he'd tried to veto. But I'd made up my mind to go ahead with this one, with or without his approval.

Take, for instance, one of my previous plans: When Danny was six, he was a chronic nose-picker. I could hardly look at him.

His finger was always up there, rummaging around, and we'd find snot smeared everywhere. So I had an idea: I would convince him that if he kept picking, he wouldn't just be digging out boogers, he'd be pulling out *bits of his brain.* I had a slew of ideas: I would drop food coloring in his nostrils while he slept, so when he woke, he would be picking out what looked like gobs of blood and gray matter. When he came to me worried, I would shine a little flashlight in his nose and recoil at the "carnage." He was learning to read, so I'd convince him of his self-inflicted harm by showing him jumbles of letters and insisting they were simple words. I even thought of loading weights in one side of his bike handlebars, then telling him he must have dug so deep he'd damaged his vestibular canals!

Of course, boring Derrick said no, and I dropped it. But not without some lingering bitterness. After that, I soldiered on for a while, nurturing my unacknowledged creativity in secret. I held my ideas close, like little suckling piglets, and hoped my imagination wouldn't wither from disuse. I silently longed for the day one of my plans would come to fruition.

So I decided: this would be the one.

Danny's fifteen now. He skateboards, plays video games, wears his pants too tight and his hats crooked. I've learned to live with all that. But what I really can't stand is the constant scowl on his face. He always looks like he's just smelled a rotten fart. It's infuriating. I've worked so hard to give him a good life, a happy life. But apparently it's uncool for a teenager to be happy and well-adjusted. Had I known, I could have saved myself a lot of trouble and just neglected him. He'd probably be thanking me now for making his angst more authentic.

So, right, the plan: inject Botox and collagen into Danny's face, so he'd wear a semi-permanent, paralytic pout. You know the saying: "If you keep making that face, it'll stick that way."

Of course, it's not true, and I know Danny's too jaded to believe it. But what if his face really did stick that way? You can't deny what's staring back at you in the mirror. Brilliant, right? And it's supposed to be relatively safe. Mort said it would wear off in six to eight weeks. And he knows Danny's oral surgeon, Dr. Kleeg. I think they're members of the Elks or something. They agreed to do the "cosmetic procedure" while Danny was under getting his wisdom teeth out, which meant there was no need to sneak into Danny's bedroom with a tank of nitrous oxide.

I was giddy with anticipation. It couldn't have been more perfect. I mean, I was a little concerned that Mort would want more than money in the way of payment. He kept hinting that this was not a "typical procedure." Meaning, I think, not legal. We wouldn't be able to pay our usual co-pay. It wasn't clear to me if he was talking about cash under the table, or sex. Turned out he meant cash. But I think I would've been game either way. Something about the conspiratorial thing we had going really got me excited. Plus, I can't deny, Mort's up-for-anything attitude was sexy. More than once, I imagined leaving Derrick for Mort and teaching Danny endless lessons together. With my inspiration and his prescription pad—just think what we could do.

Nothing ended up happening between us, of course. But a girl can dream, and a little innocent fantasizing never hurt anyone. Besides, it was just my stifled creativity running a little wild. It's like Jung said—if you bottle things up, they come out cockeyed.

Anyway, it wasn't my fault, but the plan went sideways. Derrick's never been one to say "I told you so," but if he were, he would be saying it now. The day of the procedure, Mort got sick. So he sent his colleague, Dr. Hinckley. But he knew Hinckley wouldn't be keen on The Plan, so Mort told Hinckley that Danny was short for Danielle. He said she was an 18-year-old woman, that she was squeamish about needles, and she wanted the two procedures—wisdom teeth and Botox-collagen—done at once. Danny wears his hair long and hasn't started growing facial hair, so it wasn't that much of a stretch. Not to mention he got my delicate features.

So, Hinckley went in and got ready to do the procedure. But when he looked at Mort's notes, he figured they couldn't be right. He figured, correctly, that the injections would turn the corners of the mouth sharply downward, into a perma-frown. He also figured, incorrectly, that this could not be the intended effect. So he took some artistic liberties. And he did beautiful work, don't get me wrong. But the upshot is, instead of a semi-permanent sneer, Danny got full, pouty lips and high, prominent cheekbones. I think Hinckley might have even sculpted his eyebrows.

So now Danny is confused, to say the least, and I have some explaining to do. I really don't know how to spin it. I could say the trauma from removing his wisdom teeth must have swollen his lips and cheeks. But how long could post-op swelling last? A couple weeks? And the Botox-collagen cocktail will take another month or more to leach from his system. I could tell him it's a common phase of puberty, just another in a long list of changes that he's going through. But I know what he'll say: why isn't it happening to his friends? Maybe I could find an exotic disease on the internet. Something that matches the symptoms. Something rare, but not too rare. If it were ten years ago, I could make one up. But you know kids and computers. He'd look it up and know in five minutes if I invented something.

Well. Not to worry. I will rise to the challenge. True, I'm not crazy about lying even more extensively to my son. But, on the other hand, this brainstorming is really getting my creative juices flowing. I'm feeling expressed, purposeful, actualized, for the first time in I-don't-know-how-long. You know, I really do believe everything happens for a reason.

THEOBROMA PSYCHEDELIS

The following is text from a chocolate-bar wrapper that I found in the Odsburg Public Library, folded up and wedged beneath the leg of a wobbly study carrel that was in a corner tucked away from the book stacks. The brown paper packaging looked familiar, similar to that of the Chehalis Chocolate Company, whose bars are sold at a number of local businesses, including Stardust Coffee Bar. Their extra-dark Madagascar is exceptional, should you ever come across it. But this wrapper had no logo, no brand, no insignia at all save for a small stamped image of what appeared to be a brain and two wide-open eyes. I never came across this variety for sale. If I had, I would have been too intrigued not to try it.

DARC MAJIK
ARTISAN DARK CHOCOLATE

Ingredients: Ghanaian cacao beans (74%)*†‡; cacao butter*†; beet sugar*†; Tahitian vanilla bean paste*; Kona coffee beans*‡; Brazilian yerba mate*‡; Japanese gyokuro green tea*‡; valerian extract*; Fijian kava kava root*‡; cannabis sativa oil*‡; psilocybin mushroom powder*; ground Sonoran peyote buttons*; morning glory seed*‡; salvia divinorum*; Ethiopian qat*; Thai kratom*‡; Peruvian coca leaf*‡; milled Indonesian nutmeg*‡; Turkish poppyseed*; Himalayan pink salt*

*organically grown   †fair trade certified   ‡locally sourced

EXTRA-SPECIAL LIMITED-ISSUE RECIPE

THE WORLD ON FIRE

What follows is transcribed from a field audio recording. The speaker is Ben Jemison, twenty-nine, currently of New Horizons Transitional Apartments. I happened upon Mr. Jemison in front of the Odsurg Fire Department headquarters. He paced back and forth in front of the building, speaking to anyone who would listen about his "moment of realization." He wore long, flowing, red-and-orange robes with a beaked, birdlike cowl of the same colors. A thick coating of ash covered his hands and circled his eyes. I invited him to sit down with me across the street, have an iced coffee, and tell me his story. He happily took me up on the offer.

Look, I know you're wondering why I'm dressed like this. You're thinking, *Why the robes? Why the soot? What's with the beak?* Listen, I get it. I do. Valid questions, for sure. So then, let me just explain, okay?

This all started with a surgery—a LaserTEK corrective laser eye surgery. LaserTEK being OdsWellMore's budget-friendlier version of LASIK. And sure, in retrospect this was probably not a thing to cheap out on, but hindsight is twenty-twenty, right? Anyway, I have mostly good things to say about LaserTEK. Nice people. Friendly service. Great results—mostly.

I feel like I should mention: Before the surgery, I was practically blind. I'd put in requests at the bookstore and the library for large-print texts for my lit classes. When they weren't available, I'd wear glasses and contacts at the same time, sometimes throwing in a magnifying glass for good measure.

So after the surgery, I was thrilled—the whole world snapped into focus. Really crisp, crystal clear—I can't stress that enough—it was incredible. "A total transformation of my eyesight experience," just like the brochure promised. I was amazed to discover that I could ID a familiar face from a block away. I could make out miniscule text on my tablet, fine print on a pill bottle. I could read the books I loved without straining.

But then, after a few days of reveling in this newfound ocular clarity, I started seeing spots. Or, not spots exactly. Auras, more like. Little glowing rings of light. They crept in at the periphery, and pretty soon they were popping up all over the place. I was concerned, but I kept my cool. I'd just had eye surgery. It seemed like it could be normal.

And then—what was it—maybe a week post-op, I woke up and something was different. I mean, even more different. The auras quavered and sparked. Erupted, I would say. And I saw shimmering, golden flames flickering around everything in sight.

The flames were definitely not part of the advertised experience—I could find no mention of them anywhere in the pamphlets, not even in the long list of possible side effects. And yet, there they were, looking as real and as clear and as hot as you would imagine. It was like I was in my own personal inferno—something right out of Dante.

I called Dr. Goodman, my LaserTEK Personal Eye-Care Consultant.

When he picked up, it sounded like he was eating potato chips. There was a continuous, loud munching and intermittent, foily crinkling. He said he didn't think the surgery was to blame for the flames. Out of dozens of patients, he'd never heard of such a thing. He asked me if I had any history of mental illness or hallucinations, which I don't. Then he asked if I signed all the indemnity waivers, which I had. He sounded pretty relieved about that. And then he asked how my vision was otherwise, aside from the hallucinatory flames.

I told him it was good. Really, it was great—better than great.

"Well then, Mr. Jemison, I'd have to say I count the surgery a success," he said.

"But the flames!" I said.

"Stay calm. I'm sure it'll fade. It's probably just a matter of time," he said.

He encouraged me to remind myself it was just a "minor optical disturbance." As he spoke, I glanced around the room, squinting and unsquinting my eyes. On the counter, a flame-wreathed apple blurred and refocused. *Yes*, I thought, *"disturbance" is definitely the word for it.*

Maybe it wasn't like Dante after all; it felt more like Kafka.

After I hung up the phone, I paced around my apartment—a nervous habit. I paced into the bathroom, trying to get a hold of myself, talk myself down a bit in the mirror. But of course, I wasn't comforted at all, because I was confronted by my round, freckled face, short brown hair, and sloped, bony shoulders all haloed in blazes. *Jesus*, I thought. *If seeing yourself burning alive isn't enough to scare you silly, I don't know what is.*

As the hours passed, the flames persisted, and despite Dr. Goodman's reassurances, I got increasingly edgy. I felt this unfamiliar, uncomfortable sense of urgency. I'd say it sprung from a dawning awareness of the extraordinary preciousness of time—but maybe that's getting too flowery with it. Really, it was more like every minute I had ever wasted watching bad TV—or playing mindless video games, or reading blogs, or indulging in self-obsessed fantasies—came back on me like a gas station burrito. I wondered: What had I done with my invaluable time? Where had it gone? And more importantly, what did I have to show for it?

I tried to distract myself from these thoughts by reading, but since the books also appeared to be on fire, that didn't really help. Too demoralized to resort to TV or the internet, I tried an improvised mantra:

It's only an illusion—an optical disturbance.
It's only an illusion—an optical disturbance.
It's only an illusion—an optical disturbance.

That gave me something to focus on, and it sounded soothingly officious. But the technique was flawed, because as soon as my concentration faltered and my attention slipped even slightly from those sibilant syllables, I slid back into the snug wrapping of angst that was quickly becoming my new norm. Inevitably, I glanced at one object or another—a bookshelf that blazed like a hearth, a toothbrush that flared like an oversized match—and any bit of cool, calm reason went immediately up in smoke.

That afternoon, I stood in line at GroceryPlus fretting with my shirt cuffs. To my left, racks of magazines, engulfed; to my right, cartons of candy, blazing. I had gone to the store because I usually found grocery shopping calming—there was something pastoral in the rolling hills of produce, and the long, orderly rows of neatly stacked packages had a mesmerizing effect. There's an Updike story about a supermarket, right? And basically nothing happens—even the conflict is inconsequential, and that's the point. But this time, the whole place had a fraught, frantic feeling. I ran through the store, haphazardly grabbing milk, bacon, a dozen eggs. Rushing around, I swerved to avoid a mother and her teetering toddler, and instead, Scylla never being without Charybdis, I ran straight into a large display of cereal boxes, sending them crashing to the floor.

The cereal was one I hadn't seen before, and the irony of it was not lost on me, though I couldn't appreciate the humor. It was called Toasty S'mores, and the box featured an anthropomorphic cartoon marshmallow on a stick, grinning wide over a campfire.

Of course, conceptually, I knew the flames I was seeing weren't real. But I couldn't shake the sensation. At the check stand, I couldn't understand: Why did it take such a long time to ring up a basket of groceries? And how did no one else appear to be in a hurry? In front of me, an elderly lady handed coupons to the distracted, gum-popping cashier, excruciatingly slowly, one by one. Unable to wait any longer, I abandoned my basket and left the store.

Emerging into the burning daylight, I paused for a second to consider my options. I thought about heading to Stardust Coffee Bar. I'd been working there as a barista the past two years, mornings and weekends, along with holding down a part-time graduate assistantship, slow-rolling my way to a master's in English at Odsburg College. Maybe I'd go tell my boss Terri that I quit. No more scraping by as the Bartleby of beans—I'd rather not extract another doppio ristretto; I'd rather not scrub another soy-filmed carafe. But then I found myself wondering: Why bother talking to Terri? If the flames were real, the whole place would be French roast anyway. And even if they weren't real, weren't there better things I could do? Time was wasting, and I had wasted enough of it.

Then it came to me: one thing I could do, before the whole burning world—not really, I knew—but still, maybe?—no, not really—don't be ridiculous, Ben—but, then again, possibly?—crumbled to ashes.

I headed toward my girlfriend Allison's apartment—through the center of town, past Stardust, which for the time was still standing. Picking my way along Main Street, I ducked in and out of a jeweler's, then on past Crustella's, past Anderson's and the Thirsty Dachshund, where I glimpsed the barflies on their stools sipping flame-topped schooners of beer. I turned north onto the tree-lined streets around campus: Dutch Elm Drive, Juniper Terrace, Knotty Pine Lane. I passed between green-lawned homes and the blacktop aprons of apartments. I broke from a brisk walk into a jog, into a sprint. And as I sped up, the blazing facades of the brick-and-shingle buildings roared past on either side. Up above, clusters of flame-laden clouds hung hot in the sky.

By the time I got to Allison's—panting, wild-eyed, pallid, and flushed—I can only imagine what I looked like: maybe Macbeth when he's just seen Banquo's ghost. Shivers, Allison's gray-and-white tabby, ran yowling to the bedroom.

"Will—you—marry—me?" I asked between sharp, gasping breaths.

Allison was caught off guard. She was also, to my view, caught on fire. The image was intensified by the usual sheen of her reddish curls. I resisted the urge to swat her with a blanket or push her to the floor and roll her over to smother the flames. Instead, I did what I'd come to do. I pulled a small velvet box from my pocket, opened it, and held it out. I dropped to one knee and a desperate smile seeped across my face. Allison didn't speak or blink for several seconds. Her jaw fell open to reveal a little pool of fire lapping around the edges of her tongue. Finally she spoke, very quietly.

"Benji, what are you doing?"

I told her I was seizing the day.

"Seriously," she said. "What's this about? Do you feel okay?"

I told her I felt incredible—more alive than ever! I told her that closeness to death breeds appreciation for the beauty of life. She pressed a forefinger to her lip and looked at me for another long moment.

"You're scaring me," she said. "And there's nothing in the box."

I blushed, embarrassed but not deterred, and conceded: true, there was no ring. This seemed to bring her a tiny bit of relief. At least I was *aware* that I had proposed with an empty box. I told her I didn't have time to pick a ring, but for obvious reasons (reasons that were obvious only to me, as I hadn't filled her in on my situation) I didn't want to wait any longer. I told her I wanted to do something real, something substantial. It could be the last thing I ever did. Then I added that I wanted to be a father, too, but that was more of a long-term investment, and who knew: Did we really have that kind of time? Seeing that she still looked anxious, I told her not to worry—I would get the ring later. If there was a later.

"What's the rush?" she asked. "We have plenty of time. Besides, I'm not ready."

I asked her, if she wasn't ready then, then when—*when*?

Allison shrugged.

"A couple years. After we finish school, find jobs, save a little money."

My response was not actual words, but more of a gagging sound. I meant to say that we likely didn't have that long. I decided to try reasoning with her—to help her see the light. So I told her what I saw: the whole world, consumed by flames. And I told her what it meant: our time might run out any minute. I shouted it a second time for emphasis: *any minute!*

She thought about what I said; her forehead broke into flaming furrows. Then she said she knew, in a sense, that I was right.

"As soon as we're born we start dying, right? No one knows how much time we have? Gather ye rosebuds while ye may … is that what you mean?"

But I was impatient; I could tell she didn't feel the urgency. For her it was abstract: Life is fleeting. Time is precious. For me, it was immediate and concrete: Your head is on fire. Your cat is on fire. Your neighbors' house, through the window behind you, is on fire. Nothing abstract about it. I told Allison I couldn't talk about it anymore. I needed to go. I'd had another idea.

I told her to think about the proposal. But if I'm being honest, I knew then we were through. We no longer saw things the same way. Plus, she'd never have stayed with me like this: dressed like some weird animal, standing on a street corner all day. I see myself for what I am, I really do. No job, no stability, questionable sanity. Not that different from being a grad assistant, actually.

I kissed Allison goodbye and took off down the street, back in the direction from which I'd come. I cast a parting glance over my shoulder. She stood there, stunned, flames dancing around her head like cartoon stars. Shivers crouched at her feet, fastidiously licking tendrils of fire from between his toes.

Let me say this now, to save you the trouble later: I knew my idea was a long shot—a fool's errand, really—but I had to try it. You'll laugh when I tell you. Why would it ever work, right? But think about it: If you were seeing flames everywhere, would rationality be front and center? Through such a cracked, crazy lens, even tilting at windmills starts to look sane. Judge not unless you're ready to be judged, as the flyers say.

So anyway, I ran as fast as I could back toward the center of town—my lungs and legs, like everything else, burning. When I reached my destination, I scrambled to a halt, huffing, and stared up at the face of a large, square, brick building. Two massive garage doors stood open like a pair of startled eyes.

I walked into one of the bays and reached for a gleaming chrome handle on a polished red door. Before I touched the handle, a big, meaty palm landed on my shoulder and spun me around, face-to-face with a uniformed firefighter in black boots, brown pants, red suspenders, and a blue T-shirt. His neck and biceps bulged out of the T-shirt and wisps of flame flickered from his collar and cuffs. His shirt was embroidered with the name Ted. He asked if he could help me.

I said I'd like to volunteer and asked for a tour of the station. Ted stared at me and raised an eyebrow.

I'm not a burly guy. I don't look the part of the firefighter, and even less so next to Ted, a real-life Tom Buchanan on anabolic steroids. I took a deep breath and inflated my chest to maximize my size. But as I exhaled and deflated, my heart dipped: I worried I'd lose my chance. So I told Ted I was stronger than I looked, and to prove it I proposed a bet. I bet him I could unroll a fire hose by myself, and that I could hold it steady, single-handedly, on full blast.

Ted looked at me like a horn had sprouted from my forehead. I suggested we put some money on it—a hundred bucks. He shook his hamlike head and made some pronouncements about safety. But with a little more prodding and wondering aloud what harm it could do when Ted would be standing right there, he softened. He said the rest of the crew was on a call and would be gone awhile. He rubbed his palms together and interlaced his thick fingers. Heat ripples rose from the lattice of his hands, like the shimmer above a barbecue pit. Slowly, he nodded and then gave a little shrug.

"Sure," he said. "What the hell."

Within a few minutes, I had spun the hose off the spool. It trailed along the pavement in long, cursive loops. I walked the length of it, removing curls and kinks, until it formed a straight, white line. By then I was breathing heavy and my muscles ached. I worried what would happen when the hose filled with water, but I wasn't about to waste the opportunity. I lifted the nozzle and looked back at Ted. He pulled a shorter hose from a second spool and hooked it up to a spigot on the station's wall. Then he turned a wheel on the side of the truck and told me to get ready.

"When it picks up," he said, "it's a son of a gun to handle."

I watched as the hose inflated like the world's largest water balloon. It snapped taut like a flexed bicep and immediately sprang from my grasp. As it left my hands, it knocked me on the chin. I fell back, dazed, and watched as it danced. It swayed like a drunk python, drenching whatever it faced.

At first, I was jubilant: my plan had worked! Desperate to see the flames extinguished, I followed the stream of water as it leapfrogged down the sidewalk, sideswiped a passing car, watered a row of shrubs nearby, and then soaked Ted as he scrambled to corral the hose's erratic movements.

But the flames continued to flicker, even as the water washed over them. Then, with a pang of horror, I realized the water itself was being lapped by flames. Frantically, I sprinted past soggy-burning Ted and into the bay. I grabbed a hand-held extinguisher off the wall and sprayed the sidewalk. To my disgusted un-surprise, the foam, like everything else, was coated in flame.

My plan had failed.

In the wake of it came a kind of welcome resignation. After I'd exhausted my storehouse of grasping panic—after I'd given up on trying to do anything and everything before time ran out—after the emotional storm—came an unexpected calm. I watched the wildly spewing water and the spent fizzling foam, saw Ted sprinting for the shutoff valve, and then witnessed the life slowly drain from the de-animated hose. Standing there on the sidewalk, my clenched jaw slackened, my tense arms hung loose at my sides, and my tone, my tenor, my internal temperature suddenly cooled. I thought to myself over and over:

Everything is burning.
Everything is burning.
Everything is burning.

But I no longer felt like my mind itself was on fire. I realized, yes, everything was burning—and yet, somehow, everything was not burned. Despite the flames, the world was not in ruin. The tension in my body drained further; even my eyes relaxed. My focus softened until all I could see was a big, orange blur. Then, right there on the sidewalk in the midst of everything, I shut my eyes. Behind my lids, the flames didn't follow me—not completely. Instead, they formed a burned-in afterglow, like when you've stared directly at the sun. The glow slowly resolved into a tufted crest, two broad wings, and a curling, paisley tail. Bright against black, this strange bird wafted. Its wings flapped gently, leaving their own fiery trails. And I realized what I had seen was not a world destined for the ashcan. It was a zoo full of phoenixes in all stages of death and rebirth. Everything burning, and everything forged anew from that same fire. *Yes*, I thought, *this will all give way and dissolve into flames. But it will come out, not just destroyed, but transformed.*

Metamorphosis.

A world in perpetual transition.

A great carousel of living and dying.

A truly—well, you get the point, right?

No need to beat it to death.

So I've been out here every day since, spreading that message, speaking my truth. I feel like I have no choice but to tell people what I've seen. Such a beautiful image, isn't it—full of pathos, but also filled with hope? It really highlights the beauty and the fragility and, ultimately, the resilience of life. Or something like that.

DOUBT CLUB

The following is a reprinted facsimile of a flyer that I found on a community bulletin board at Stardust Coffee Bar.

Stardust's owner, Terri Newsome, and her wife, Ailene, roast all the beans on site, so the space is always toasty warm and suffused with nutty, chocolaty aromas. That, combined with the constant low hiss of steam wands and the hum of espresso and coffee machines, could put a person right to sleep. It was not uncommon to see someone yawning and nodding at a table or at the bar along the counter with a laptop open or a book splayed before them—caffeination notwithstanding.

While the overall aesthetic of the place was rather spare— white walls with a few framed photos, polished concrete floor, brushed metal furniture—the back wall was painted matte black and dotted with a large mural of constellations, which I found to be an excellent canvas for idle contemplation.

I attended one of the meetings advertised on the flyer below, but you will not find an account of that experience, mainly because I did not learn anything at the meeting that was not conveyed at least as concisely by the flyer itself.

?????

COME ONE, COME ALL TO THE

EXISTENTIAL DOUBTERS' NONDENOMINATIONAL DISCUSSION HOUR

Every Thursday evening at 7:00 p.m. in the Floris and Dev Rothman Memorial Room at the Odsburg Public Library, join us for the Existential Doubters' Nondenominational Discussion Hour. Despite what you may have heard, we are not a religion. **We are NOT A CULT.** Comparisons have been drawn between Existential Doubting and, for example, Atheism, Unitarianism, and Agnosticism, just to name a few. But Existential Doubting is not any of those others. It is different. Come see and experience for yourself.

OUR CREED

We PROFESS that we don't have a clue as to:

1. Where we come from,

2. How we got here,

3. Why we're here now, or

4. Where we might go afterward.

We AGREE to continue wondering, both in solitude and in the context of fellowship, what on earth this whole fiasco called "life" is all about.

All are welcome. Come for fellowship and conversation, stay for light refreshments. Every meeting ends with Q & no A from 8:30 to 9:00 p.m. Stop by and feel the wonder!

ALPHA, BETA, DELTA, THETA

The following was shared with me by a pregnant woman who happened to be sitting near me one afternoon at Stardust. It is possible she saw my audio recorder and mistook me for an investigative journalist. Then again, she may have just identified me as a friendly looking stranger with a ready pair of ears.

She said the experience described as follows took place at a free clinic offered by the experimental medical technologies division of OdsWellMore, presumably the same division responsible for LaserTEK. She said there were rumors that the division was a joint venture of OdsWellMore and a Seattle tech company called Numeric. The primary-colored "N" logo had supposedly been spotted around town—on wallet cards glimpsed when paying for coffee, on polo shirts under plain black fleece jackets, on travel mugs in consoles of unmarked cars, and so forth. I was unable to confirm or deny these suspicions.

In fact, I could not even find the offices or facilities of OdsWellMore on my own. A former employee, on condition of anonymity, once drove me to the gates of the company's white-washed concrete compound, which sat at the end of a long, unmarked road outside of town. I walked the last half-mile to inquire at the guardhouse (the employee did not even wish to be sighted in the vicinity), but I was not admitted in. Although I did a fair amount of poking around, I was unable to locate the road again.

The woman here said she and her husband signed an extensive confidentiality and nondisclosure agreement prior to services being rendered, which again attests to the company's secrecy. However, the experience was evidently sufficiently remarkable to her that she felt the need to tell someone, and I happened to be in the right place at the right time. Unsurprisingly, she declined to give her name.

"Watch the monitor and you can see what your baby is dreaming."

The technician—a tall, dark-haired woman about my age in a crisp lab coat and pink scrubs—said it matter-of-factly, like she was talking about the weather. We'd been given no sense of what to expect before we arrived. My OB had referred me for what she called a free supplemental prenatal screening. I figured why not, if she was recommending it—the more information we had, the better.

"Wait, what?" I said.

The tech smiled this benign kind of half-smile, pulled a flatscreen down on a long swivel arm from the low, paneled ceiling of the dimly lit room, and placed it in front of us. I was leaned back in the exam chair with my T-shirt tucked under my breasts. She sat next to me, gliding a gray plastic puck across my belly.

The screen flickered, then glowed solid white. Then there were images, abstract at first, pulsating washes of color. Sounds, too—like air gusting through a tunnel. Then, slowly, the colors shifted to familiar forms: an elephant, an oak tree, a curled-up cat.

"I can't believe this," my husband said.

His eyes were wide. He wasn't blinking. Of course, common sense said our daughter, in the womb, had never seen any of those things.

The technician smiled, a big, eye-creasing smile this time, but stayed focused on the screen. She said it was real, strange as it seemed. Something about collective consciousness, or embedded genetic memory. I thought it must be exciting getting to show this to people and see their reactions, but then I noticed she wasn't looking at us at all. She looked as mesmerized by the screen as we were.

The sound changed then, from white noise to murmuring voices—mine and my husband's.

Soon there were more images: a fish thrashing in a net; a flock of seabirds in flight; heavy storm clouds gathering; a child throwing stones; a train trailing a plume of smoke; fruit piled in a basket; a screen door casting a long shadow.

"How does it work?" I asked.

The technician still hadn't turned from the screen, and she answered without looking at me.

"The sensor detects alpha, beta, delta, and theta waves in your baby's brain and the computer deciphers them as images and sounds. Not so different from a radio or a TV, just signals received and translated. Deceptively simple."

I nodded.

"Sure," I said. "Simple."

I looked at my husband, but he wasn't listening. His hand was on my shoulder and his face was covered in tears. I looked back at the screen. It had returned to abstract shapes and swirls of color. I laid my hands on either side of my belly, took a deep breath, and shut my eyes. When I opened them again, the screen was blank and the tech was typing something on a tablet. I cleared my throat, and she seemed to have just remembered we were there. She flicked on the overhead lights, gave us a nod, and we were ushered quietly out, just like nothing had happened.

CEASE AND DESIST

The following is a reprint of a letter, on 8½ in. × 14 in. legal letterhead, very serious and official-looking, which was slipped under the door of my apartment shortly after I spoke with the aforementioned pregnant woman. I cannot say I was entirely surprised by the letter, nor did it deter or distract me in any way from my work.

One thing I have learned during my time as a socio-anthropo-lingui-lore-ologist is that people are unsettled by observation, which is why I try to make myself as inconspicuous as possible. However, in a small town it seems nearly impossible for a newcomer to go unnoticed.

Correspondence such as this does cause me to pause and consider the motivations of the sender, or of the sender's proxy, as it were. Why would they be so concerned with my presence? What did they have to hide?

In the spirit of transparency, and in the name of independence, I feel compelled to mention that I did not use the coupons referenced in the letter, so as not to allow the slightest taint, or even the mere appearance, of a potential conflict of interest. It is of utmost importance to me that my accounts are my own, unvarnished and uninfluenced by anything but my own unavoidable personal lens.

The coupons, as I recall, included such enticements as a free latte from Stardust, a buy-one-get-one domestic draft at the

Thirsty Dachshund, a complimentary appetizer from the Goose & Gander, and half-price nachos at Anderson's Tavern—items of interest, certainly, and they spoke (perhaps too knowingly) to my desire to save a few dollars and keep overhead low. Nevertheless, I remained steadfast and refrained from redeeming even one.

I would have liked to have included the coupons here for reference, but unfortunately I seem to have failed in my preservationist duty in this particular instance and misplaced them—another artifact sadly lost to the eyes of future historians.

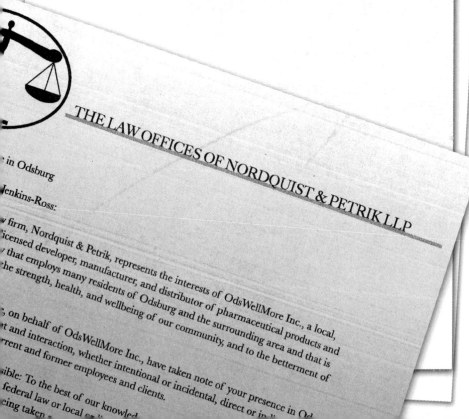

THE LAW OFFICES OF NORDQUIST & PETRIK LLP

in Odsburg

Jenkins-Ross:

firm, Nordquist & Petrik, represents the interests of OdsWellMore Inc., a local, icensed developer, manufacturer, and distributor of pharmaceutical products and that employs many residents of Odsburg and the surrounding area and that is the strength, health, and wellbeing of our community, and to the betterment of

on behalf of OdsWellMore Inc., have taken note of your presence in Od and interaction, whether intentional or incidental, direct or in rent and former employees and clients.

ible: To the best of our knowled federal law or local ing taken

From the law offices of Nordquist & Petrik LLP
RE: Your time in Odsburg

To Mr. Wallace Jenkins-Ross:

Greetings! Our law firm, Nordquist & Petrik, represents the interests of OdsWellMore Inc., a local, longstanding, fully licensed developer, manufacturer, and distributor of pharmaceutical products and services—a company that employs many residents of Odsburg and the surrounding area and that is deeply committed to the strength, health, and wellbeing of our community, and to the betterment of humanity as a whole.

Please be advised that we, on behalf of OdsWellMore Inc., have taken note of your presence in Odsburg and your engagement and interaction, whether intentional or incidental, direct or indirect, with the company and/or its current and former employees and clients.

We wish to be as clear as possible: To the best of our knowledge you have not, as of this time, done anything illegal under state or federal law or local ordinance. You are not being charged with any crime, nor is any formal legal action being taken against or served upon you.

Nevertheless, we are aware of your activities, and should you conduct any business or commit any action that constitutes an infraction of any applicable law or ordinance, or that infringes or impinges upon the business of OdsWellMore Inc., including protected trade secrets or intellectual property, we and our representatives and assigns will take any and all necessary and appropriate actions, to the fullest extent possible under the law, to protect our client's business interests.

As you are a guest here in Odsburg, and as we are sincerely concerned with the safety of all those who step foot in our beloved town, we certainly would not wish that any harm should befall you as a result of any ill-advised actions that you might choose to take. Therefore, we would like to politely recommend that you tread lightly, so to speak; that you stay on the beaten path; and that you refrain from anything that might endanger your safety or the safety of others.

We would like to further remind you of the many fun-filled activities and charming local businesses that Odsburg and the surrounding community have to offer, and we encourage you to spend your limited time here in a way that is enjoyable and relaxing. In this spirit, we are enclosing several coupons for generous discounts at some of Odsburg's most beloved establishments, as well as trail maps for day hikes in the beautiful wilderness areas nearby and a free pass for a Sillagumquit River rafting trip. We hope you will accept our warm hospitality and make good use of these gifts.

If you have any questions or concerns, or if there is any way in which we may be of service to you, please do not hesitate to contact us. We truly do wish you a pleasant stay here in our town, however long or short it may turn out to be.

Best,
Lewis Nordquist, Esq.
Principal and Partner, Nordquist & Petrik LLP
Enc: Coupons

DEAR DIARY

The following are extracts from diary entries believed to have been written by Mary Elizabeth Ods, the wife of town cofounder Josiah Ods. From what I can gather, Mrs. Ods's disappearance after her husband's death was a topic of speculation among her contemporaries, and evidently still interests local history buffs.

I heard one theory that Mrs. Ods traveled abroad, studying in various spiritual traditions, only to return years later under the name Alva Moonstone (when discussing the town's tendency toward odd and unexplained happenings, Ms. Moonstone's presence and ascendance is another factor residents cite). Mrs. Ods would have been in her sixties or seventies by the time of Ms. Moonstone's arrival, which agrees with the historical accounts—not that this is proof of any kind, but the timeline fits the narrative.

The original documents are among the papers of the Odsburg Shadow Historical Society, which is housed in a small, sublet storage area in the third-floor attic of the public library building, directly above the offices of the official Odsburg Historical Society, which declined to comment on these documents, and which I was told places the highest value on certifiability—to the exclusion, it seems, of highly interesting materials such as the ones that follow. Though their provenance is admittedly unverified, to my eye the papers looked authentic.

I was fortunate enough to view and hand-copy the documents below after I became fast friends with the self-appointed chief historian of the OSHS, Martha Robbins, thanks to—what else?—a shared affinity for collecting and preserving otherwise-shunned historical castoffs.

While not strictly on topic, I feel it bears mentioning that Ms. Robbins made the best banana-walnut-chocolate-chip muffins I have ever had the privilege of sampling.

12th November 1855

His eyes. I cannot find the words to say what I mean precisely. His eyes still have dark crescent moons beneath ~~them~~ gaze straight through aught earthly set before him. But seems so clear that he is seeing something. Thought I saw him reach out with an arm. Perhaps to point a finger at it to stroke it with his ~~hand~~ palm. Whatsoever it is, seems ~~that~~ I shall never know.

15th August 1855

Not long in this place, new home bearing our name, Jh. grown strange. Eyes foggy, half-blank, mind wandering Lord knows where. Not like him, but does no good to dwell upon, too much work to do & with no help. (Knitting, darning, washing, cooking, tending our tiny flock.) What little fortune we had now gone, what choice? What choice but to bear up and do the work of two? Arms strong from chopping wood, carrying water, tilling this patch of borrowed—stolen—earth. Don't mind work, but I worry. Worry the water put some sickness in him. Something in the foodstuff, some forage he found, berries or bark. Worry when, whether will pass.

21st August 1855

Last night woke to bed empty beside me, door ajar. Peeped out to find Jh. full dressed, muttering in a tongue I could not recognize. Leaves in hair, soil beneath fingernails. Been outdoors, doing what I cannot guess. Not planting nor gathering, surely. (Forgive my better nature overtaken by bitter tone. I came along here willingly, true enough, and know that whatsoever I get here, I shall own.) He neither saw nor heard me. Took myself back to bed, but could not rest my mind. Find I cannot settle what to feel: anger, fear, or sorrow. Waited for first light to stoke the fire, put the kettle to boil.

29th September 1855

Jh. much worse. Moans in otherworldly way. Neither animal nor
man he sounds like, but some spectral thing. Trembles as if with
fever, but cool to touch. His brother stopped coming 'round.
That so-called doctor Bemis good for nothing. Says only, "Give
him rest." Says his spirit must be tired. He no longer eats & ribs
show through his vest. Dark half-moons have bloomed beneath
his eyes. Can't hardly sleep. Like caring for a newborn babe,
which now I think it, he is so much like. Except I cannot lift nor
soothe him, nor wrap or rock or nurse him, to cure whatever
ails him. Suppose it wrong to say, but I thank the Lord he did
not see to bless us with a brood. Each time I bled again, I cried
& surely felt bereaved, but now can only feel relief. Not for lack
of love, but could not care for children and my husband now.
They say more hands for working but I never saw it so. And Lord
forbid those never-children showed what ill is in Jh.'s blood.

22nd October 1855

He brought me here, then left me. The words repeat unbidden.
I tell myself he did not choose to leave me, but still curse him
for it. He sits there on a stump all day, makes nary a sound.
Facing the wood, but would wager my life, whatsoever it be
worth, he sees not a thing—not trees nor sky nor ground nor
me. I bring him food, as always—bacon, bread—he stares right
through. Lord help me, I had hoped to find some peace here
in this place, now we were settled.

12th November 1855

His eyes. I cannot find the words to say what I mean precisely.
His eyes still have dark crescent moons beneath & gaze straight
through aught earthly set before him. But seems so clear that
he is seeing something. Thought I saw him reach out with an

arm, perhaps to point a finger at it, to stroke it with his palm. Whatsoever it is, seems I shall never know.

1st December 1855

Jh. is passed, gone to the Hereafter, whatsoever it may be. Suppose I ought feel more grief, except he left me long ago & I have already mourned. Never did return to himself, not properly. Did say something near the end. Looked at me—square in my eyes—first time since I remember. Said, "Don't we all … don't we all." Know not what it meant, nor if he said all that he meant to, or was leading to something more.

1st January 1856

Cannot say what I ought do now. Jedediah says they could take me in—him & Delia, that dour wife of his, their roiling crop of children. Could stay, grow old, a widow graying in their kitchen, an extra pair of hands to mend their socks. Feel more a pull to go off on my own. Know not where, nor what for, but think I shall go. We were only ever squatting here, at best. Tell the truth, I am no fool. I'll wait for spring thaw. Sooner would be foolishness. While I miss Jh., need not join him straightaway. When weather turns mild, shall pack a few things, quietly, & leave. Nothing at all holding me here.

A VISIT WITH ALVA MOONSTONE

What follows is transcribed from memory from a pilgrimage I made to the purported grave of the faith healer Alva Moonstone, who, as previously noted, may or may not have been known at one time as Mary Elizabeth Ods.

I had identified one of Ms. Moonstone's followers, long-locked and Birkenstocked, smoking something fragrant and loitering outside the library with a far-off stare. He told me his birth name was Seth, but that his spiritual name was Ganymede. After I told him of my work, he agreed to escort me to the site, which was a fair walking distance into the woods at the eastern edge of town.

When we reached the place—a small, mossy bower containing a rough stone altar festooned with colorful flags and climbing, flowering plants—Seth/Ganymede poured me a cup of some type of strong tea from a striped thermos, then invited me to sit and listen, and said Alva would speak if she desired. As I sat, I entered a kind of trance. I closed my eyes and I could still see the sunlit clearing around me. I sensed, though I could not see, a figure sitting nearby. I heard a voice, warm and soft as a pair of woolen socks, that came to me as if through a long tunnel, as if carried a great distance on the wind.

After I woke from the trance, some thirty minutes later by my watch (I lost all track of time during), Seth/Ganymede escorted me back into town, and I joined a group of Alva's devotees for a delicious dinner of freshly baked bread and a vegetable stew. Her followers, at least those I met, were unfailingly warm, welcoming, and kind, albeit a bit spaced-out—not too dissimilar from any of the townsfolk, I suppose. I remain grateful for and inspired by their openness and hospitality.

Child. My dear child.
I am so glad to see you.
So glad you've come to visit.

We have known each other forever.
But I've not seen you in such a long time.
How in the world has it been so long?

My darling one.
You already know everything I could tell you.
But I will tell you anyway.

From the womb of the earth you were born.
And back into the womb you will return.
Waveform rising from ocean's surface—
glancing about, flailing, mustering motion and sound—
before curling over and falling back into the wider water.
Re-emerging, reabsorbed.
Ever so.

Once you were a priestess.
Once you were a penguin.
Once you were a pomegranate.
You have been so many, many things.

Nothing is truly new.
Every life another turn of the infinite, spiraling coil.

Once you were my mother, and I was your baby boy.
Once we were lovers, and we have killed each other, too.
Over eons, we have been all to one another.
All of us have, each to the next.
Nothing new, and all exists between us.

Nothing ever new, never new, nor ever can be.

Just that our memories are short, and remembering takes work.
And oh, how we dislike work.

So instead we spin our webs again.
Going through the motions.
The same familiar patterns.
Neurosis as inheritance.
Reincarnation of our weaknesses and fears.
The deepening grooves of habit.
Our flaws in photonegative, knowing only what we wish not to be.

Remember you have choices, more choices than you know.

And remember, too:
Everything is borrowed, nothing owned.
That includes your time, each moment in this bodily form.
Use it wisely.

Take care of yourself.

Take care of those around you.
Nurture and be nurtured.

Each and every other is yours, and you are theirs.
Breathing a common ether, bleeding a common blood.
Organs within one body.
Vessels, ventricles, veins.
Parts of the whole, inseparable.
Flowing together, co-belonging.
Remember that, my child, if you remember nothing else.

Go now.
Go on.
We will see each other again.

A WOMAN WALKS INTO A
BAR AND THE BAR TOP
SPARKLES WITH PROMISES
UNTOLD. THE WOMAN LOOKS
AROUND AT THE BEAUTIFUL
STRANGERS. THE BARTENDER
NODS, HE'S WRINGING A
TOWEL, SAYS, "WELL, WHATCHA
DRINKIN'?" AND THE WOMAN
GRINS WIDE, AND HER
PEARLY TEETH GLEAM LIKE THE MOON.

A WOMAN WA
AND SITS DOWN
A WOMAN
HER AROUND SO SHE IS
FACE-TO-FACE WITH THE NEAT
ROWS OF BOTTLES, THE WHOLE
HOLY CHORUS OF BROWN-AMBER-
OCHRE-GOLD-YELLOW-CRYSTAL.
ON EACH PAPER COASTER A
GLASS THUNKS AND TINKLES
WITH ICE-ANGEL MUSIC. SHE
SHOUTS "AMEN."

A WOMAN WALKS INTO A BAR

What follows is a collection of writings that I found left behind on the bar at the Thirsty Dachshund. The words were scrawled in small block letters in black ballpoint on a stack of cocktail napkins, etched with as much effort, from the look of it, as the initials, slogans, and epithets carved into the wooden bar top itself.

The napkins were neatly arranged in front of the seat customarily occupied by Carla Tharpe, forty-five, with whom I shared more than one drink on more than one evening over more than one bowl of heavily salted yellow popcorn from the machine in the Dachshund's dark front corner. I asked Carla later whether she had written them, but she neither confirmed nor denied it. She shook her head, gave me a long stare, and said, "I really don't remember."

A WOMAN WALKS INTO
TRIES TO WALK INTO A
BUT THE DOOR WON'T S
OPEN, SHE TUGS BUT IT'S
LOCKED AND SHE SQUINTS
HER PHONE, CHECKS THE H
THEY OPEN AT NOON, SHE
COULD SWEAR IT WAS NOON,
SHE CURSES THE DOOR AND
CURSES THE WORLD A
THE DRUMS

A man walks into a bar and says—wait, stop. Why a man? Why is it always a man who walks into the bar? You never hear "A woman walks into a bar." But why not? It's about time somebody started a story with "A woman walks into a bar," don't you think?

A woman walks into a bar with a duck. The bartender nods at the duck, then says to the woman, "Hey sweetheart, what'll you have?" She bristles at "sweetheart" but orders a beer and the bartender brings her a pint and the check and the duck says, "Enjoy your drink, babe—I've got the bill."

A woman walks into a bar, sees a priest, a rabbi, and a Buddhist monk, and at first she thinks, *Shit, I walked into a church*, then she sees that they're drinking and sighs with relief and slides onto a stool, gets a bourbon, and listens a bit to their god conversation.

A woman walks into a bar and the bar top sparkles with promises untold. The woman looks around at the beautiful strangers. The bartender nods, he's wringing a towel, says, "Well, whatcha drinkin'?" And the woman grins wide, and her pearly teeth gleam like the moon.

A woman walks into a bar and birds chirp, flowers bloom, little chipmunks jeté, and the bartender lands from a neat triple lutz, softly plunks down a glass, fills it up, slides it over—the drink pirouettes to slap five to the woman's raised palm and all's right with the world.

A woman walks into a bar and sits down. The stool spins her around so she stops face-to-face with the neat rows of bottles, the whole holy chorus of brown-amber-ochre-gold-yellow-crystal. On each paper coaster a glass thunks and tinkles with ice-angel music. She shouts "amen."

A woman walks into a bar, in her throat the crisp-cold, in her brain tingly-warmth, and she thinks *first-sip-best-sip* but amends and then counters *next-sip-best-sip*, so she orders another ten minutes another ten minutes another and on just like that all night long.

A woman walks into a bar the sensation that builds in the backs of her eyes ocean-swells she thinks *this is the place where I surf* two more drinks she thinks *please god don't let the crest break* two more drinks she thinks *god help me just let me drown.*

A woman walks into a bar stalks into a bar tumbles into a bar fumbles into a bar ambles into a bar gambols into a bar rambles into a bar shambles into a bar putters into a bar stutters into a bar mutters into a bar gutters into a bar huddles into a bar muddles into a bar scuttles into a bar.

A woman walks into a bar and she thinks to herself, *It's not safe, it's not safe, no I know, I will stop, for my health and all else, yes I know, yes I'm lucky, of all that could happen, could've happened already, to put myself into this kind of position, I know I know better, I'll stop it, I will.*

A woman walks into a bar can't remember where was it she came from did she have an appointment or something or somewhere to be was it maybe a job interview can't remember *ah fuckit* she thinks *be here now* and she calls down the bar for another.

A woman walks out of one bar to another but did she remember to close out her tab can't remember and wait did she have one more card and where did that forty bucks go but she thinks *oh forget it it's gone c'est la vie* and she smiles at a neighbor just neighborly-like.

A woman walks into the floor, at least that's how it feels, she remembers her foot reaching down from the rung of the stool and then *smack* she remembers the smash of her nose and her lips on the lacquered wood planks.

A woman walks into a bar keeps her gaze off the mirror she's looking real hard the other way she pretends not to see herself looks at the floor keeps her eyes on her shoes keeps her hands on her purse and her lunch she keeps down but just barely she thinks *goddammit you brain shut up.*

A woman walks into a bar and she's chuckling alone she's the only one laughing at a joke in her head it's so funny she can't help but laugh someone asks "What's so funny?" she just stares ahead, thinks, *Well shit, you don't get it, then I can't explain, it's just life, life's a big fucking hell of a joke ha ha ha.*

A woman walks into a bar, sees the bartender talking, sees everyone talking, but all she can hear is the wind in a tunnel, or sounds bubbling up from a lakebottom dredge, it's all in slow motion with everyone's voice like an off-tune bassoon through her ears cotton-plugged.

A woman walks into a bar, tries to walk into a bar but the door won't swing open, she tugs but it's locked and she squints at her phone, checks the hours, they open at noon, she could swear it was noon, she curses the door and curses the world and curses the drums in her head.

A woman walks out of a bar, stumbles out mumbles out bumbles out humbles out crawls out falls out bawls out stalls out oozes out woozes out snoozes out dribbles out quibbles out snivels out shrivels out pisses out bobbles out hobbles out wobbles out, out into the blinding sun.

VISCERAL

The following is transcribed from a field recording. The speaker is a man I encountered sitting on a wrought iron bench in the town square. He identified himself only as "Phil," and I could not pin down his age with any accuracy. My best guess would be thirty-five, maybe forty. He was rail-thin and had a shock of dark hair that hung down to his eyes. He appeared at first glance to be wearing a grayish-brown felted sweater-vest, but upon further inspection, it turned out that his torso was coated in a thick layer of lint and other light debris. Later, when I asked other residents about Phil, they typically cringed in recognition and said they knew him as "that strange skinless guy." Later still, I learned there was a period when I was widely known as "that blinking, bearded, bespectacled fellow with the notepad and audio recorder who seems to think he's blending in." People call it how they see it, and they never see the whole picture, do they?

It started as a small slit: just a little opening in the skin, right at the center of my sternum. I spotted it in the mirror. I was standing over the sink, shaving before work, and there it was, like a new mole or an ingrown hair, only … weirder. Of course I was concerned but, to tell the truth, not really alarmed. More curious than anything.

I didn't go to the emergency room or call my GP. None of the things you think you'd do if something odd like this were to happen. Not that you ever expect something like this to happen, exactly. But I think you know what I mean.

For a while I waited and watched, too interested to do anything else. As I stood there, observing, the opening didn't bleed, didn't pus, didn't ooze; it just slowly grew wider.

An hour later, I sat down in my cubicle in a quiet, fluorescent corner of the OdsWellMore corporate office, where I worked in promotions and outside sales. I put on my headset and autodialed the first number on my list. Then I delivered the spiel and half-listened to the person on the other end of the line. By then the small slit had opened into a rounded diamond shape. I thought about a card within a deck, shuffled and frayed and scuffed against others. My mind wandered and returned.

Every so often, in the middle of a call, or in the brief moments between, I unbuttoned my shirt to peek in. Each time I could see the patch of bone, the geometric plane growing as the skin peeled away.

By dinnertime, I could see the curved slats of several ribs, glistening in the glow of the fixture that hangs above my kitchen table. The skin had receded over most of my chest and was continuing its slow, steady retreat. It crept around my sides and across my back. I watched the intercostal muscles between my ribs stretch and relax with each inhale and exhale. But this was the most striking thing: without those seven layers of skin, and the subcutaneous fat that went with it, there wasn't as much padding to muffle the sound of my heartbeat, which thudded audibly in the quiet room.

I reflected on what a thin and vulnerable membrane the skin is to begin with. Then I had this funny thought: *skin is overrated.* I had to laugh a little about that. And yes, I know skin protects us from infection and generally holds us together. I try to be grateful. But isn't it, in some sense, a hindrance? Isn't it a false, or at least misleading, boundary line? One that we too willingly accept at face value?

I thought about messiness and interconnectedness and books I'd read about Buddhist and Christian monks and nuns, about Hindu holy people and Yogis all over the world, about how this is really, on some level, what they're all talking about. Isn't it? At least, sort of? It's not unrelated, anyway. And I thought about how really, fundamentally, we're not separate to begin with. We can't possibly be. So who needs skin?

Besides, by late that evening, the wound had stopped spreading. That is, if you could even call it a wound, neat and clean and bloodless as it was.

At that point, my entire upper torso was exposed. It was disconcerting, but really only in a tentative, cringe-y sort of way. For a minute, I worried about the lint and other debris that would collect on the soft, moist flesh between and around my ribs. On the slick, exposed surfaces of pectoral, abdominal, deltoid, and trapezius.

But then I thought, really, what would be the harm? If I'm to be one with the universe, that means being one with the couch fibers. One with the carpet fuzz and the cat dander. One with the particles and plaster dust and fumes and grit and grime.

Let it in, then, I thought. Why not? Let it all in.

A DOUBTER'S PRAYER

The following is a reproduction of a leaflet I picked up from a table, among a handful of other handouts, alongside coffee urns, Styrofoam cups, cookies, and donuts, when I attended a meeting of the Odsburg Existentialists In-Dependence recovery and support group, a separately run offshoot of the aforementioned Existential Doubters. The group is not unlike Alcoholics Anonymous or Narcotics Anonymous, but does not distinguish between different types of addictions, dependencies, or substances, nor—as one might guess—does it definitively acknowledge that addictions, dependencies, or substances necessarily exist.

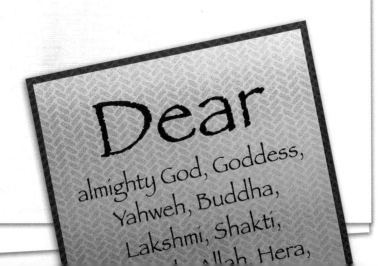

Dear

almighty God, Goddess,
Yahweh, Buddha,
Lakshmi, Shakti,
Allah, Hera,

Dear almighty God, Goddess, Yahweh, Buddha, Lakshmi, Shakti, Jehovah, Allah, Hera, Aphrodite, Krishna, Ganesha, Tara, Maya, Vishnu, Rama, Hecate, Metztli, Jah, Hashem, Kuan Yin, Elohim, Earth Mother, someone else, or possibly no one:

I recognize the awesome power of your omniscience—if you do exist—and the all-too-poignant contrast between that omniscience (if indeed such omniscience is truly possible, and if in reality you possess it, because, after all, could there not be a godhead figure that is still fallible and limited in its knowledge?) and my own lack of certainty about anything at all.

Further I acknowledge the utility and purpose, if not the absolute or verifiable truth, of the Bible, the Torah, the Talmud, the Kabbalah, the Zohar, the Qur'an, the Vedas, the Vedanta, the Brahmanas, the Aranyakas, the Upanishads, the Tantras, the Sutras, the Yogic texts, the Tipitaka, the Abhidharma, the Mahayana, the Kojiki, the Tao Te Ching, the Book of Shadows, the Odu Ifá, the Tibetan and Egyptian Books of the Dead, the Popol Vuh, *Cat's Cradle*, and any other text that might help us to find the strength and resilience to be kinder to ourselves and to others, to forgive and have compassion, to consider things from an alternate perspective, and to at least think twice about how our actions are working to create our own happiness or misery, as well as impacting those around us—that is, so long as the text is not misinterpreted, misapplied, or bent toward the unethical aims of some unscrupulous individual and/or organization.

Moreover, I admit that I have a problem—which we may call an addiction, dependency, vice, or any other name, without changing its essential problematic nature—and that this problem stems from my relationship to what we, in this plane of existence in which we temporarily cohabitate, call substances, and from the fact that I have—as each of us here has—used one or more of these substances in such a way as we call misuse or abuse.

I confirm that my use of such substances can rightly be called a problem because, indeed, it has caused problems, and I say this knowing full well the intractable stickiness that surrounds the concept of causation (and the dictum that it is not to be conflated with mere correlation) and the difficulty—if not impossibility—of proving that any one thing truly causes another.

In this rare and exceptional case, in these extenuating circumstances, I am willing to suspend the strictures of doubt and disbelief—after witnessing such a close and undeniable correlation, on so many discrete and sequential occasions, between my substance use and subsequent undesired outcomes—and declare that my use of such substances has caused—yes, *caused*—problems.

And I further definitively declare, in a rare flare of decisiveness, that these problems my problem has caused can rightly be defined as problems, with no doubt whatsoever, based on the negative and undeniably problematic consequences that they have wrought in my life and in the lives of those nearest to me.

And even if in the end it were to turn out that *drugs* do not really exist per se, and even if *I* do not really exist, and even if *you*, God et al., do not exist, nevertheless I can point to those problems that my substance use has caused and say: "Yes. I see them. There they are. They are problems."

And from this harmoniously conflicted place of overwhelming doubt and uncharacteristic certainty, holding the two in tenuous but somehow comfortable balance, I reach out for support.

I reach out to my community of fellow doubters, whom I shall not doubt are here for me.

I reach out to my friends and to my family, insofar as I am able and they are willing.

I reach out to any of those texts aforementioned, and any others not mentioned, that might give me strength and hope and guidance.

I reach out for whatever stable surfaces might help to keep me upright and moving forward in a world—if indeed this is a world in which we live—where everything seems so crumbly and chimeric and questionable—and I do hereby solemnly swear that when I reach out, it will not be for those slippery and sinister substances that, while they may seem to offer some momentary buoyancy or anchor, in the end will only capsize this little lifeboat adrift at sea.

SPINNING JINNIES

The following story is transcribed from a field recording. It was spoken by one of the town's several resident clairvoyants— Rhonda Lifschitz, sixty-eight, of the Odsburg Gardens Apartments (but, she said, originally from Centralia)—whom I met at the aforementioned gathering of Alva Moonstone devotees. Her reputation for accuracy and insight is all the more impressive given her reasonable rates.

She had the widest, greenest eyes and the longest, whitest hair I have ever seen, and sitting near her felt much like sitting in a patch of afternoon sunlight. Before recounting the story, she took several deep breaths, assumed an unblinking thousand-yard stare, and then spoke in what I can only describe as the manner of a grandmotherly robot, if that robot were receiving a live satellite feed from a newsroom stationed in the future.

Odsburg. Six months from now. After several rounds of arduous lobbying by OdsWellMore, along with an extensive PR campaign of postcards, placards, and bus ads promoting Local Proposition 2, all pharmaceutical testing and sales regulations are provisionally lifted. Prescriptions and patents for all types of medication become unnecessary. After a brief period of confusion and distrust, market activity erupts.

A staggering number and variety of medications flood the market. The old standbys—painkillers, antidepressants, antibiotics—remain available, joined by myriad additional compounds only lab rats have tried. No prescriptions or physicians' notes are needed. Everything is over-the-counter, at the nearest gas station or corner market, while supplies last.

Ethical debates rage. Some people tout the change as a beacon of a new chemical utopia. Others tell cautionary tales of people going mad on unregulated drugs and killing or maiming their friends, relatives, and neighbors; or, if not that, then killing themselves with the untested toxic compounds. The municipal government, for its part, decides to let the whole thing play out as a grand libertarian experiment. The town council members fold their hands and issue a blanket warning of *caveat emptor*. Rumors circulate that the mayor is addicted to Odscodone, but in truth his pockets (and the pockets of several council members) are lined with cash from OdsWellMore's coffers.

Two weeks after deregulation, a tattooed "pharmacist," who until recently had been called a bartender, leans across the polished zinc counter of Anderson's Tavern, rests his weight on his elbows, and waits for Agnes Blinn to make a decision.

Agnes, twenty-six, bored and bemused, just off a shift waiting tables at the Silver Spoon Diner, perches on a swiveling stool, wiggling her toes inside her shoes, looking up at the menu scrawled out on a chalkboard.

Frog Whompers.

Clear Blue Skies.

Apple Brown Betties.

The names are whimsical and evocative, and not at all informative. She considers just ordering a beer instead. She considers requesting a recommendation. She considers turning around and leaving empty-handed. She reads the list again.

"Okay," Agnes says. "I'll try the Spinning Jinnies."

The pharmacist ducks into the maze of bins and canisters behind the counter, and after much rustling, scraping, and tapping, he returns with a small white paper bag.

"Twenty bucks," he says.

Most of the drugs cost twenty dollars. Most of the business is in cash. Despite deregulation, people feel uneasy about paper trails.

"Twenty bucks," Agnes echoes.

She hands over a twenty and walks away carrying the little white bag. She takes it to a park a few blocks over, sits down on a wooden bench, and lifts out a small brown glass bottle. She thinks about the fact that it would probably be safer to sample a new drug in the comfort of her home, but she weighs that against the pull of the outdoors, the draw of earthy expanse, and she stays there, seated on the bench.

Agnes twists open the white cap of the small brown bottle and shakes two pink tablets into her palm. The bottle only contains two tablets, which Agnes infers is the dose. She pops them in her mouth, swigs from her water bottle, swallows, and waits.

For a few minutes nothing happens. Then, slowly, the leaves on a nearby maple tree start to spin, catching the wind like thousands of little pinwheels, picking up speed until the whole top of the tree becomes an enormous, whirling green mass. Agnes shakes her head, and the blurry mass burns a windsock trail. She turns her gaze down from the tree and finds it is not just the massive maple that's spinning. The blades of grass at her feet are tiny flagellate turbines spinning separately and in tandem, creating a pulsating, undulating carpet of green. When Agnes blinks, another layer of the fabric rises into view. She sees not just the leaves and the grass spinning, but the cells of the plants themselves vibrating, jumping from their places and refusing to stand still. As she watches, the paler green of the grass bleeds into the deeper green of the leaves; the dirt-brown of the path seeps into the bark-brown of the maple trunk; and her own clothes and skin begin to throb and swirl, right down to the blue buttons on her yellow wool sweater.

Through all of this, Agnes is breathing. She breathes and the world around her breathes too. She draws the scene down into her lungs, and the scenery absorbs her. Eventually, there is just breath and swirling color and Agnes's abiding awareness. And then there is just awareness itself—no more Agnes. At that moment, all the weight of human existence evaporates. At that moment, all self-conscious murmurings dissolve into the humming of a hammer-struck gong. And at the very next moment, the Spinning Jinnies wear off, and Agnes Blinn is back on the park bench, back to herself again.

Agnes continues to breathe, to feel the gentle rise and fall of her abdomen, chest, shoulders, and she realizes that she is *not* actually, or not fully, herself again. She has left some portion of her worldly weight inside the swirl of colors and vibrations. In doing so, she has retained some lingering magic of the entrancing, oscillatory whirl. And then slowly, quietly, she raises herself from the bench and begins her walk home.

Twenty-four hours after taking the Spinning Jinnies, Agnes Blinn becomes permanently and completely blind. First colors fade to gray, then shapes blur and go soft, then finally the light dims and everything goes black. OdsWellMore denies responsibility for this outcome, as they do with all drug-related incidents. They insist that when regulations and controls were lifted, all adult citizens of Odsburg implicitly took upon themselves any risk of injury stemming from any substances they might choose to consume, and all prior contracts, guarantees, and claims of safety became instantly null and void. Agnes nevertheless files suit against OdsWellMore and settles out of court for an undisclosed sum. She is seen frequently thereafter walking in the village with a guide dog named Rufus. Observers often remark that they move as if one. And Agnes, her eyes unreadable behind dark glasses, responds:

"But don't we all?"

PLEASE KEEP SMILING

I recorded the following in the long, echoing, linoleum-tiled hallway of Odsburg Elementary School. I was waiting to give a short presentation about my work to Jenny Loomis's fifth-grade class when the speaker—a small, fidgety girl with a long strawberry-blond braid—stepped out of the line of her peers, walked up to me, and began talking. She was still speaking at a good clip when a hall monitor arrived to usher her back to her classroom.

Hi! What's your name? My name's Libby. I'm five and a quarter. I'm in kindergarten, in Miss Graves's class. Yesterday was report card day. It was my first one. Do you know about report cards? When you're a big kid like me, and you're in kindergarten, your teacher sends a report card home to say how you're doing. It comes in a scratchy mustardy-yellow envelope. The paper inside is light pink, like bubble gum, and so thin, like a butterfly's wing, or like tissue paper, the kind you cut up and crumple to make flowers with pipe cleaners for stems.

So I got on the bus with my bubble-gum report card inside its mustard envelope inside my unicorn backpack and thought about a unicorn eating a mustard and bubble gum sandwich and it made me laugh because that is silly. I told the bus driver and she smiled and told me, "Find a seat, hon." I felt big and important and the bus went rumble-rumble and I bounced on the green plasticky seat next to Robbie. Robbie's in my class. Do you know Robbie? Robbie had chocolate around his mouth and boogers in his nose and I wondered if that was on his report card. Do you know what goes on a report card? I checked my nose for boogers and felt my mouth for chocolate but I didn't find any.

When the bus got to my stop, I bunny-hopped down the stairs. Mom was waiting in our house. Our house is a few houses down from the corner where the bus stops. I hoped she would read my report card and say what it said. I can read a little but not cursive and not a lot of words so I could only read it if Miss Graves printed the words and used small ones like "cat" and "sat." When I got home I took off my sneakers and went to the table and told my mom it's report card day. Mom said she knew and I wondered how she knew and I wondered what other things she knew about school that I hadn't told her and I wondered if she and Miss Graves talk on the phone late at night the way Mom talks to Aunt Kim, swashing a cup of her purplish juice and laughing and crying and yelling.

I pulled the report card out. It was still in its envelope. I handed it to my mom and asked what it said. She read it then smiled big and gave me a hug. She said Miss Graves said I'm a pleasure to have in class and well-behaved and play well with others. My mom was happy and it was 'cause of me so that made me happy, too. It made me feel fuzzy like I was snuggled in a sleeping bag watching cartoons and eating cereal, which is the best feeling. So much better than when Mom is sad or mad. I can tell the difference 'cause it feels different like the playground feels different than the principal's office. Mom said when Dad got home he'd have a surprise.

When Dad got home he brought the surprise and it was a little ice cream cake like I got on my birthday but smaller. Dad looked happy too. They were happy and proud and said I did a good job and I felt warm and Miss Graves thinks I'm a super student and they're smiling at me and I love that feeling, I want to keep it and hold it, keep them smiling at me so I have to be really good I have to play nice and be a pleasure and get right answers on spelling quizzes and do good drawings and everything really good so my mom and dad and Miss Graves will keep smiling not crying not yelling not sobbing not sad, so I feel like I'm swinging on my favorite swing eating clear gummy bears which are the best because they taste like pineapples but if Mom and Dad and Miss Graves are sad or mad I lose the feeling and I don't want to lose it I really really don't and I think, *Keep smiling at me, please, don't be sad or mad anymore, I'll do anything please I'll be so so good, I'll do everything right and never make mistakes, I promise, cross my heart, hope to die, stick a needle in my eye, just keep smiling, just please please please keep smiling ...*

GREAT ASPIRATIONS

The following document is a typed reproduction. The original was handwritten—or, rather, scribbled—in red crayon on a piece of yellow construction paper. The heading was done in black felt pen in neat block letters. I found it on a bulletin board in the hallway of Odsburg Elementary. I must confess: I intended to return the original document after transcribing its contents, but I unfortunately never got around to it. I'm sorry about that.

Miss Melton's Second-Grade Class   Career

"What I Want To Be When I Grow Up"   By Ton

**Miss Melton's Second-Grade Class
Career Week Projects**

"What I Want to Be When I Grow Up"
By Tommy Anderson

- a dragon
- a dinosaur
- a dolphin
- a superhero
- a king
- president
- a football player
- a fireman
- a lawyer
- a project manager
- a self-starter
- goal-oriented
- results-driven
- highly organized
- a strong multitasker
- proficient in Microsoft Office

HYPOTHETICAL

The following is a transcription of an interview with Dewey Morgan, a gangly, freckly fifth-grader at Odsburg Elementary. The recording was made in conjunction with a presentation that I gave to Jenny Loomis's fifth-grade class for their cross-disciplinary pedagogical unit on ethnography, anthropology, and oral history.

I told the class a bit about my discipline, and about the basic human need to tell our stories. I shared with them that, when interviewing, I like to begin with a simple, open-ended prompt, such as "Tell me something about yourself," or "Is there a story you'd like to share?"

When I called for a volunteer to demonstrate, Dewey's hand was the first to shoot up, and it turned out he needed no prompt at all: he marched to the front of the class and launched directly into the following story about his friend Colin, who was also in the class, and who declined to be interviewed other than to say, "Yup, that happened."

So Colin asks me, "If you could have lunch with anyone living or dead who would it be?" And I say, "Wouldn't you choose someone dead 'cause I mean come on wouldn't that be amazing to bring someone back from the dead, wouldn't that be wicked, you couldn't pass that up, but wait would they still be dead but dug up and woken up, like would they be all gross and worm-eaten and rotten or would they be like regular alive and healthy 'cause that makes a difference, or wait what if you choose someone dead but you didn't realize you have to die to have lunch with them and then it's too late to change your mind because you already made your choice and you're dead now in the afterlife, or wait how 'bout this what if you choose someone historic like Abraham Lincoln or Paul Revere or Gandhi but you don't specify what age to bring 'em back and you find out you're having lunch with 'em as a baby so all you're doing is spoon-feeding 'em pureed peas or giving 'em a bottle and yeah sure it's them but really it's a baby so what's the point right so maybe I should just have lunch with somebody living instead, like a movie star or supermodel, but jeez how intimidating I'd be too nervous and prob'ly embarrass myself and what would we even talk about so maybe I'll just choose you Colin that sounds pretty good, yeah do you want to eat lunch with me?" And Colin shrugs and shakes his head 'cause I definitely missed the point but he's like, "Okay sure yeah whatever Dewey let's eat."

TOMWABFAM

I found the following document, discarded or forgotten, on a molded plastic bench in the waiting area of the Odsburg High School administrative offices. I was there to apply for a job I saw posted in a classified ad for a part-time custodial assistant (another attempt to earn some extra cash, though this one unsuccessful, as it seems I was bested by a competing candidate with more applicable experience). Nevertheless, I always try to find a silver lining, and in this case that lining is the document that follows. The original appeared to have been torn along a perforated edge from a standardized test booklet.

This section will test your reading comprehension.

Read the passages below and then answer the questions that follow.

The old man with a beak for a mouth was not always an old man with a beak for a mouth. At first, he was neither old nor beaked. At first, he was a poor baby without any mouth at all—born with no lips, no jaw, no tongue, and no teeth.

The poor baby's parents, shocked and dismayed, were offered a bird's beak to replace their son's missing mouth. The beak would come from a South American parrot called a scarlet macaw, and the transplant would be done by a very well-paid doctor called an orthopedic surgeon. The parents were nervous, but hoped to give their boy a chance at a "normal" life, inasmuch as that was possible.

The transplant succeeded, and the poor baby without any mouth at all became the incredible baby with a beak for a mouth, who, in turn, through the steady, inexorable wearing of time, became the old man with a beak for a mouth about whom you are reading today—a man who has lived a long, productive, and yes, "normal," life.

The old man with a beak for a mouth has a proper name, too. His name is Gregory. But people don't call him that. Instead, they call him TOMWABFAM (or TOM for short), which is an acronym: a word formed from the initial letters of a phrase or series of words.

The above definition was paraphrased from Merriam-Webster, a popular producer of reference materials. *Merriam* is a homophone of *Miriam* and *marry 'im*, as in the following example: "Did you hear about TOMWABFAM? *Miriam*, the old lady who sells dried flowers, says she will *marry 'im* next summer. Have you seen them walking hand-in-hand? They are a sweet pair."

Of course, TOM would not have told you any of that, because his beak-mouth is busy clipping and crimping sheets of tin. TOM makes many things out of tin: tin snowflakes, tin lamp shades, tin ceiling tiles, tin candelabra, tin masks, and tin cups, among others. He sells these items at flea markets and craft fairs all around the tri-town area.

In addition to tin, TOM has a fondness for gin. Gin is liquor

1

CONTINUE

made from juniper berries. And "fondness" is an understatement. Maybe it was the trauma of a childhood full of ridicule, or the loneliness that stemmed from an inability to kiss and court young ladies when he was in high school. Or maybe it was a genetic tendency too eager to express itself. Whatever the reason, TOM became dependent on gin to get through the day.

As a younger man, TOMWABFAM (then TYM-WABFAM) had a family. He met a woman who loved him, despite—or perhaps even because of—his beak-mouth, and they were married and had two normal-mouthed children. But even back then, his drinking was a driving wedge that pushed them apart, until his wife finally left and took the kids to live with her parents in Ohio. He's rarely seen them since—though he does send cards and tin-cut trinkets from time to time.

These days, TOM can often be heard singing to himself, a bouncy-sounding tune about snipping tin and sipping gin. Some might say TOM is in denial. Some might note that the edges and etchings on TOM's tin items are shakier, more uneven, than they used to be. Some might observe that TOM packs up his market stall as soon as he's collected enough cash for a bottle. And some might speculate, reasonably, that TOM will die a premature death (though not all that premature, considering he is an old man, and how long can old men expect to live?) from cirrhosis of the liver.

When TOM dies, his epitaph could read: "GREGORY (TOM-WABFAM) / A MAN WITH A BIRD'S BEAK AND A LION'S HEART," with the bird's beak being literal, and the lion's heart being a metaphor for courage. Because, alcoholism and familial abandonment notwithstanding, TOM must be courageous—mustn't he?—in a way?—to have persevered such as he has.

If nothing else, one may imagine—and be heartened by the thought—that should TOM predecease Miriam (TOLWSDF), his grave will be beautiful: decorated, year-round, with a blanket of dried azaleas, marigolds, and tulips.

2

CONTINUE →

Now that you have finished reading the passage, answer the following questions:

1

Define, in your own words, the following terms: transplant, inexorable, acronym, homophone, candelabra, tendency, wedge, cirrhosis, persevere, predecease

2

What is a scarlet macaw? Where does it come from?

3

What does the acronym TOMWABFAM stand for?

4

How, exactly, did the poor baby without any mouth at all become the old man with a beak for a mouth? Are they the same person? Or has the passing of time (and repeated replacement of each individual cell) remade them as separate and distinct individuals, several generations removed from one another, connected only by those mysterious and elusive (illusory?) qualities we call "memory" and "identity"? Answer in metaphysical terms.

5

Do you think what Gregory/ TOMWABFAM and Miriam/ TOLWSDF share could be called "True Love"? Do you think such a thing as "True Love" is possible, or is it a misleading (and even potentially damaging) mythical construct? Do you believe you have experienced it? If so, describe.

CONTINUE

AEOLUS

The speaker is Carlie Hewlet, eighteen, a senior at Odsburg High School and the only daughter of Lorna Hewlet, a professor of poetry at Odsburg College. I recorded what follows from her recitation at an open mic at Stardust Coffee Bar. She seems to have a knack for the family craft.

I should note here, too, that there are some ramifications for copyright and fair use, given that what follows is a creative composition. However, I trust—as I often must—that a combination of attribution and good intention will win the day.

My girlfriend Sam—she's twenty-one, three years my senior, now three times a senior, soon to graduate into the world if all goes well—came loping out from shady woods, so tall and lean and lined with dirt, and tumbled cackling in the grass, her flannel shirt and canvas pants spread-eagled by the chain-link fence behind the salmon cannery where we had spent the afternoon in smoke and idle thoughts. She'd disappeared among the pines an hour before without a word; she re-emerged a haggard mess and grinning ear to ear.

"What happened to your face?" I asked.

She sputtered, busted-lipped and bleeding: "Carlie, I've been hugging trees."

I turned one eyebrow up to make a question mark.

"And also berry bushes, clouds and rocks and dirt and streams."

Before I got the chance to ask her what she meant, she stammered on:

"I've been cut up and bashed against and scraped and scratched and clawed, and what I figured out is every mark's a marker of relationship: these bruises black tattoos of leaning-in—each rising welt a lipstick kiss—and every drop of blood that leaves me, well, it doesn't really leave at all but just extends me out, flung farther, wider to the world."

She paused. Her eyes were wild and white. She blinked—
and then continued on:

"We're always breathing. Have you ever noticed that? We're
always breathing, everywhere: our lungs, our skin, our cells,
and not just that—we're always drinking, eating—ingesting
and excreting—absorbing and diffusing—and aggregating and
disintegrating, growing up and growing out and sloughing
off and—god—it's happening all the time! We build imaginary walls, we tell these stories all about how all alone we
are—how separate from each other—right? We build and
build, and then at once, it all evaporates and there you are:
you're standing in the midst of everything, and you are everything, and stranger yet, you aren't even you—or not yourself
alone—because you're in this conversation, see, this constant
and unstoppable exchange; you can't hold on, you can't hold
back, you can't maintain your little stash of life—it's like the
universe in uniform is at the door, it pounds a meaty fist, it
yells to you: 'Come out! Surrender now!' But—oh!—you're
so afraid. 'No, anything but that,' you say. 'I can't let go of my
identity, my separateness, it's all I have!' But, ultimately, even
that you never really had, because the Universe Police? They
don't give up, they never rest, and in the end your hands give
out and you relax your grip—release the faded armrests of
your easy chair and recognize you're nothing but a conduit, a
circuit board, a hollow reed, a bamboo shoot the universe is
flowing through—it's not a perfect metaphor, but do you get
the gist, at least—?"

I looked at her: her eyes held stars, her mouth a crescent
moon. And then her face became my own, and I was pretty
sure I knew exactly what she meant.

DEEP-SIX

The following was spoken by Odsburg College poetry professor Lorna Hewlet, referenced in the introduction to the preceding document. I collected the recording one night while wandering the college's academic halls, looking to see if, by some vanishingly small chance, the school might have a department of socio-anthropolingui-lore-ology, or, if not, then perhaps an oral history department, or even an interdisciplinary concentration in interpretive storytelling. No such luck, on all counts.

I paused when I heard Professor Hewlet's voice, a soothing murmur, coming through her slightly open office door. She was leaning over her laptop, tapping erratically as she spoke, so it is possible she was drafting or reciting from upcoming, unpublished work. If this is so, I place myself at the mercy of Professor Hewlet's goodwill and understanding, and that of her potential publisher, once again on the basis of attribution and intention. If nothing else, perhaps this citation could serve as some small form of free publicity, for while I am no book critic, I think she is quite good.

... why else would you find yourself awake at 3:00 a.m., your pupils bathed in bluish glow, perusing and erasing search results for *how to self-induce a fatal heart attack*, if not to spare your husband and your teenage girl the hassles heaped on suicide survivors—endless, dim *what-ifs* and *why*s and *what-could-I-have-dones*—if not to give them, and yourself, postmortem, all the benefits, the dignities accruing to a *natural* demise—in light of which they'll be allowed to feel their shock and sadness unalloyed—their righteous, cleansing anger leveled squarely at the universe, and/or at their respective gods, unsmudged—and spared unhappy, fruitless speculation as to what exactly might have been so awful in this quiet, privileged life that you'd be eager to engage that ever-long ejection seat, to jettison your soul and end your days before your stamped expiry date—plus the nuisance of insurance claims investigations ... best to spare them that as well, if possible, and see that they're provided for without the contestations, protestations, probate snags and such—and yes, of course, there could be other ways to go—like maybe in an *accident* instead—a certain gawkish, bleak allure; a grim and somber flair—but don't those single-car collisions, don't those arcing falls from shaky ladders, don't those skydive/hang-glide/parasail *mistakes* always strike you as a little fishy—don't they leave the aftertaste of doubt—and so, so much the better if it looks as if your body turned against you, mutinied, because who'd ever will that fate upon herself—who even *could*—and so, who'd ever even question—question, even for a moment, ever—whether there was any cause to cast suspicion on your tragic, early death?

Actualyze

will teach you
to remove
&/or destroy
your physical
& psychological
blockages
to achieve
personal growth
& fulfillment.

Want to know more
of course you do.

Let me ask you:
What is keeping you
from growing into
your dreams?
From growing into
the person
you want to be?
From growing into
destiny?

ACTUALYZE

The following is a typed reprinting of a handwritten artifact. The original was written in blue ballpoint on a length of receipt tape, gone pink at the edges from activated toner. It was rolled tightly into a tiny scroll, with a thin, brittle rubber band wrapped around the middle. I found it in the pocket of a faded brown suit coat on a sale rack at the back of the Go-Around-Again second-hand store, a place I frequented perhaps more than necessary, both for a bargain and because it felt like a spiritual home: a cluttered treasure trove of the chipped, faded, and fraying, the lovingly worn—a staging ground for countless items as much in need of care, as deserving of another life, as the stories and artifacts collected here.

In addition to a fast fondness for the store itself, I felt a kinship and commonality of purpose with its proprietress, a stooped-over, soft-spoken woman named Miriam, who appeared every bit as devoted to her castoff menagerie as I am to this bedraggled bundle of wayward words. She seemed to perpetually inhabit a cloud of dried-flower fragrance that my admittedly amateur nose identified as violet, begonia, and chrysanthemum.

Hello Friend.
Let me tell you
about Actualyze.
Actualyze is not
your typical
self-help program.
Actualyze is
a revolutionary
Self Actualization
System.
Actualyze
will teach you
to remove
&/or destroy
your physical
& psychological
blockages
to achieve
personal growth
& fulfillment.
Want to know more?
Of course you do.
Let me ask you:

What is keeping you
from growing into
your dreams?
From growing into
the person
you want to be?
From growing into
your destiny?
Look at it this way:
your destiny
is a pair of pants
3 sizes too big.
What are those
3 sizes?

1.
Your own
limiting beliefs
about what you
are & are not
capable of.

2.
The limitations
imposed on you
by those around you.
What your family,
friends & coworkers
tell you every day
about what you can
& can't achieve.

3.
The limitations
inherent in
humankind's
imperfect
scientific knowledge
& unrealized
technological
capability.

Here's the
good news:
Actualyze can
help you
transcend
&/or obliterate
all 3 major
self-realization
obstacles
& grow into
the oversize
pair of pants
that is your destiny.

"How?" you ask.
Thru a combination
of hypnotism,
hallucinogens,
& daily affirmations.

So: do you want
to shrink

your destiny-pants
to fit the small,
limited,
blocked-up self
that you are,
or do you want
to grow
into that destiny
handed down
by generations
of humans
who made
your life
possible,
& realize
the limitless
greatness
of your
full potential?

The choice
is yours.

But before you
walk away
from this
opportunity,
remember:
There are only
3 things
standing
between you

& your fully
realized potential:
1. Your own
limiting beliefs.
2. The limiting
statements
& beliefs
others direct
toward you.
3. The limited
advancement
of science
& technology.

In other words:
1. Your beliefs
2. Their beliefs
3. The absence
of mind-reading
robots

Or,
even more simply:
1. You
2. Them
3. The fact that you
do not possess
a time-traveling
jet pack

Its simple as that.
So, do you want

to remain
the undeveloped
nobody you are,
or do you want
to time-travel
into a glorious,
utopian future?
Do you want
to live
the ho-hum life
you know,
or do you want
to zoom
thru the universe
on a jet pack
w/ a clairvoyant
android companion
named Vivien
who understands you,
truly understands you,
bcause she can hear
your every thought?
Which will it be?
If you want to make
the right choice
& grow into
your futuristic
jet-pack-robot
destiny pants,
you will sign up
now
for the 2-day

Power Seminar
& get yourself
started on the path
to mind-boggling
personal growth.

By the end of
the 2-day seminar,
you will have
set aside
&/or incinerated
obstacles 1 & 2
& you will be
well on your way
to overcoming
&/or eviscerating
obstacle 3.
& if you can
accomplish that
in 2 days,
imagine
what you can do
w/ the rest
of your life!

You owe it
to your current self
& also to
your yet-unrealized
possible future self.
Because if the pants fit,
wear them.

& the clothes make the
man &/or woman.
So do it.
Sign up.
Destiny.
Pants.
Robots.
Future.
Jet pack.
Actualyze.

CAT GAME

I witnessed the following events while hiding in a decorative hedge positioned conveniently in the elaborately landscaped and meticulously manicured front lawn of the home where the interaction took place.

It was one of the larger estates in town, set back a bit from the road, on a good half-acre plot—a true rarity—in the middle of River View Drive. A nameplate on a carriage lamp near the front steps said "Mund."

To the fullest extent possible, the interaction is recreated here just as it happened, except where I couldn't hear exactly what was being said, in which case I took minor artistic liberties and filled in the blanks in a way that seemed most contextually plausible.

Regarding the recurrence of the term "Actualyze," I would like to be able to shed some light for you, Dear Reader, on the relationship between the previous artifact and Mr. Llewellyn. Believe me, I tried to trace such a connection. However, I did not manage to track down Mr. Llewellyn after this encounter, nor was I successful in seeking out further information on the Actualyze program—its origins, provenance, and so forth. And so it remains a mystery, unelucidated, one of many.

"Silk. Silk. Silk."

Reginald Llewellyn—earnest, stout, balding—stood on the steps of 4052 River View Drive rubbing his tie between his fingers and repeating the word quietly. The smooth sensation and soft sibilance appeared to calm him while he waited for someone to answer the door. After a few moments he heard footsteps, and a well-dressed middle-aged woman appeared in the doorway, framed as though she were in a portrait and made up as though she had commissioned the portrait herself.

"Hello," she said. "May I help you?"

"Yes, ma'am," said Reginald. "My name is Reginald Llewellyn, and I'm here representing Actualyze: The Self-Actualization System. Do you have a few minutes for my time—I mean—may I have a few minutes of your time today?"

"I don't know," said the woman. "I'm *very* busy."

Her tone dripped with sarcasm, but Reginald caught only the bare, literal meaning of the words. So he said, politely, "Very well, ma'am. Thank you anyway. Have a nice day."

He turned and plodded down several of the terraced steps.

"Not so fast, Reggie," the woman said. "May I call you Reggie?"

"Sure," said Reginald.

"Reggie, I was joking with you," she said. "I have plenty of time. Talk your head off if you want. I have nothing I need to do and I could use some entertainment."

"Oh," said Reginald. "Then allow me to inform you about Actualyze: The Self-Actualization System!"

He straightened his tie and re-climbed the steps.

"May I ask your name, ma'am?"

"It's Kitty."

"Glad to meet you, Kitty. Are you familiar with Actualyze?"

"Let's say I'm not." She inclined her head toward Reginald. "Tell me like I've never heard of it before. Describe every detail."

"The first thing I should tell you," he said, "is Actualyze is not a political or religious organization."

She pursed her lips and furrowed her brow, a caricature of someone listening.

"It is a transformative self-development program designed to bring about a radical inward revolution."

Reginald accompanied this statement with a series of grand, stiff-armed gestures—first out around him, and then in toward his heart.

Kitty leaned against the doorframe, folded her arms, and nodded.

Reginald had brought with him a small rolling suitcase, which he unzipped, removing a deflated punching clown—the kind that, when inflated, will rock to the floor when struck and spring back up. He bit the nozzle and began to blow into it, filling the toy with air.

"Do," said Reginald, between breaths, through clenched teeth, "You. Ever. Feel. Like. One. Of. These?"

He continued blowing until the clown was a symmetrical egg shape, then set it down at Kitty's feet.

"All the time," she said. "Sometimes my husband does too—if he's lucky."

"And are you happy with that? Feeling like a punching bag, there to be smacked around for everyone else's amusement?"

Reginald paused for effect, then punched the clown for punctuation. Kitty opened her mouth to make another joke, but Reginald carried on.

"Of course you aren't," he said. "You want to feel more like this."

He reached again into the suitcase and pulled out a plastic mask: the face of a tiger. He placed it over his face and secured it with an elastic band.

"You want to be commanding, powerful, assertive!"

His words were muffled through the mask; he sounded like the disembodied voice of a fast food drive-through. He prowled around the porch, swiping at the columns with his hands, growling to display confidence and dominance.

"You're right!" Kitty said. "I do want to feel like that. Show me how, Reggie."

Reginald reached into his bag once more, groping this time, his vision obscured by the mask. At last, he produced a pamphlet and, fumbling, pressed it firmly into Kitty's shoulder, then her forearm, then her hand.

"This is how," he said.

"A pamphlet is how?"

"The pamphlet describes the system. And tells you how to sign up."

"I see," she said. "Now, about this—Reggie, I have a question."

She leaned in close and stage-whispered into the ear of the tiger mask.

"Could you be persuaded to be my personal teacher in this Actualyze Self-Actualization System?"

"Oh," said Reginald. "I don't think so. I'm new myself. Not qualified to coach. I'd need to unleash my own tiger before I could help you with yours."

Kitty leaned closer still, her lips grazing Reginald's ear.

"I'd like to help you unleash your tiger, Reggie."

He took a small step backward.

"That's nice," he said. "But it's not about you helping me—it's about you helping yourself."

Kitty appeared dumbfounded: how dense could he be?

"May I ask you something, Reggie?"

"Sure," he said.

"How old are you?"

"Thirty-one."

"And have you ever been with an older woman?"

"Older than what?" he asked.

"Older than yourself, Reggie."

"Oh," he said. He thought for a moment. "No, I suppose not."

He was still wearing the tiger mask. She reached out, pulled the mask from his face, leaned in, and kissed him on the mouth.

"I—" he said.

His eyes were wide, his mouth ajar.

"How was that for empowerment?"

She licked her lips and squinted.

"I—I don't know," said Reginald. "I don't think that's what the program is about."

He began rubbing his tie between his fingers again.

"Reggie," she said. "How would you like to come inside and have a drink? My husband's not home, won't be 'til late. I promise, before you go, I'll sign up for your program. And you might leave feeling empowered yourself."

Reginald continued to fumble with his tie. A bead of sweat trickled down his temple. In his eyes, she could practically see the flashing reflections of sheer lingerie and satin sheets. He fondled his tie and repeated to himself, silently this time: Silk. Silk. Silk.

"All right," he said.

He took a tentative step forward, then another. His right hand reached for Kitty's left breast; his mouth gaped slightly. She stood perfectly still, watching him closely. She must have seen the fearful wonder in his eyes. Then she took two quick, padding steps backward into the foyer of the house, out of his reach. Reginald's left foot landed on the welcome mat, then his right. He stood teetering at the threshold.

"Thanks, Reggie. It's been fun!"

She swung the door shut between them. The snap of the deadbolt echoed off the concrete pillars. Reginald stood with his hand still raised, reaching toward the heavy front door, his mouth open. His gaze dropped to his feet. He should have known better. He reached to pull the tiger mask from the top of his head, intending to pack his bag and go. The only thing his fingers touched, though, was a patch of thinning hair, and he realized he'd been robbed; she had the mask in her hand when she retreated into the house. Not only had he made no sale, but he was also out one tiger mask. He sighed heavily through his nose and his thick shoulders slumped forward. Behind him, on the steps, the punching clown was slowly deflating. It, too, made a sighing sound from a little hole where the air leaked out.

LATE BREAKFAST AT THE CORVAIR

What follows is transcribed from a field audio recording. This story was related to me by Evan Lindstrom, twenty-four, over pancakes at the Silver Spoon Diner, which I have been instructed to tell you is no substitute for the far superior Corvair Diner, which is sadly no longer in business.

I understand, from general conversation, that the two diners had fiercely loyal clienteles and served as the locus and focus of a (mostly) friendly rivalry while both were in operation. It seems it was not uncommon for devoted patrons of one institution to hurl food at the rival establishment's façade with the intention of startling unsuspecting patrons quietly dining behind the windows.

However, that brand of lighthearted rivalry seems quite out of place in my interview with Mr. Lindstrom, given the gravity of what he wished to recount. As he spoke, his eyes were contemplative and sad, two polished stones peering out between shaggy brown bangs and incipient beard. He was dressed in a rumpled powder blue oxford and pleated khakis that somehow, in themselves, evoked a sense of bereavement. Or maybe I was projecting that last part.

The baby showed up on a Wednesday—same day I found out my Uncle Jim was dead. Died unexpectedly in his sleep. Myocardial infarction, the coroner's report would say. Heart attack. He was fifty-three.

On the phone, after she broke the news, my mom said something about arrangements. Gave the name of the funeral home—Roberts or Robards. I had a hard time focusing. After a few minutes, neither of us knew what to say, so we said goodbye.

I left my apartment that morning in a stupor. Got to work—in admissions over at Odsburg College—without any memory of the trip. Worked all day in a fog. Typing absent-mindedly. Daydreaming through meetings. Staring at a cup of pens. Trying and failing to glean any meaning from application files, enrollment reports.

Everything reminded me of my uncle. My boss clapped a colleague on the back, coach-like: I remembered Jim on the sidelines of my Little League games. A crumpled sheet of paper brought to mind the lines around Jim's eyes, creases from constant smiling. A car engine revving in the parking lot—even that made me think of him.

Jim, I should say, was more like a dad to me. When I was a baby, my dad disappeared. Not magical-mystical disappeared. Mom said his car was just gone from the driveway one morning. For years after I first heard the story, engine noise made my heart skip a beat. But Jim—to hear my mom tell it—never skipped a beat. Stepped in as honorary dad as easy as most people step into their shoes. He and my Aunt Helen hadn't been able to have kids, so I guess he was glad for the opportunity.

Eventually, I associated a car engine with Jim. He'd drive over from Klester for any reason, or none at all. I remembered, with a mix of fondness and sadness, trips we took to Mount Rainier, a Mariners game, the zoo in Portland. Jim was there for birthdays and graduations. Showed up to family day at my school when my mom couldn't get off work.

Memories shadowed me through the day, crowding out any functional thought. At one point, I made fifty copies of a blank sheet of paper. Only back at my desk did I realize what I'd done. I stood to return the stack of paper, then sat back down. Picked up a pen, pulled a sheet off the stack, and wrote in big block letters:

Breakfast w/ Uncle Jim. Friday. 8:00.

Our monthly ritual. It was two days away. We'd have met at the Corvair Diner, where we'd each get two eggs, bacon, toast, and coffee. We'd catch up, reminisce, just sit. Watch the sidewalk traffic. Watch the waitresses with their loaded trays. Watch the sunlight crawl across the Formica tabletop. Watch an over-easy egg or a syruped pancake slide down the plate glass as the Silver Spooner who threw it ran away laughing.

The last one was the last one, I thought. Had I known, I would have remembered it better. Would have remembered Jim better. Would have absorbed the details, even inconsequential ones. The sound of spoons rattling in coffee cups. The squeak of the vinyl booth seats. The smells of syrup and butter as plates wafted by. The way Jim gestured with his fork and cup as he talked. The way he dropped food and sloshed coffee.

If I'd known, I would've held onto it. If I had, maybe I could reconstruct what I'd lost—perfectly, precisely. That's all I wanted: I wanted the past, wanted it now, wanted it always. Wanted it stashed in a box where I could pull it out, open it up, and live it in three dimensions and five senses. Was that so much to ask? Was that so unreasonable? So unachievable? What would it take?

I spent the rest of the day in my cubicle, entranced. I imagined coming here, to the Spoon, toting a whole case of eggs, but the thought held no joy. Instead, I re-read emails Jim and I had exchanged. Looked through old photos on my phone—I had a steady stream as my mom and Aunt Helen had both started digging them up and sending them along. Taking in the language and images, I tried to recreate his presence. I hoped by consuming and digesting the words, pictures, memories, I could revive the reality. Bring him back. I left the office after dark, exhausted and disappointed.

When I got home, there was a basket on the doormat in front of my apartment. A condolence gift, I thought: a wicker boat of fruit and candy with a sympathy card ribboned to the top. *We Are Sorry For Your Loss. Time Heals All Wounds.* Whoever sent it, it was nice. But a part of me wanted to drop-kick it down the hall. I unlocked the door and picked up the basket. It was covered with a powder blue cloth, so I couldn't see what was inside, but it had heft that shifted when I lifted it.

I tossed my keys on the counter and bent down to see what the basket contained. After I peeled back the cloth, it took me a second to realize what I was seeing: a small blue knit cap, two neat little rows of eyelashes, a tiny nose, two fists hardly bigger than walnut shells, a pair of fleece booties—my god! It was a tiny person. A baby, that was the word.

I set the baby, asleep in its basket, on my bed. I didn't think this was something that happened, people leaving infants on doorsteps. It was like I'd stepped into a made-for-TV movie. I didn't know what to do with a baby—what to feed it, how to change it. Why would I? I was an only child, I never babysat, I don't have kids. But there I was. What to do?

Probably, I thought, I should call Child Protective Services. But they'd have their hands full. This baby would get shuffled around, not get proper attention. Who knows what would happen to it? So it wouldn't hurt to take care of it for a little while. I'd be doing everyone a favor. Just a little while. Why not? I could use the company. I could use the distraction.

I told the baby—who was still out cold—that we were going to the store. When I got to the GroceryPlus, I took a cart and set the sleeping baby, still in the basket, inside. I didn't know what I was looking for. Formula? And if I needed formula, I also needed bottles, and diapers—and what else? Baby powder, ointment, wipes. At the checkout, I dumped it all on the belt.

The cashier was a teenager. Her nametag said "Judee." She peered at the baby and cooed.

"Is that your son?" she said. "He's adorable."

"Oh, yeah," I said. "Thanks."

"How old?"

"Um," I said. "Three months?"

She looked surprised.

"He's pretty teeny for three months. Still all pink and wrinkly."

"Did I say three months?" I backpedaled. "He's three weeks."

Judee watched me a moment. I was afraid she'd call over a manager and bust me. I wondered what the penalty was for not turning in a lost-and-found baby to CPS. I wondered whether parents carried proof of guardianship for babies, like car registration.

"He's a cutie," she said.

I thanked her, swiped my card, and headed out the door. One arm full of grocery bags, the other holding the basket by its woven wicker handle.

At my apartment, I unpacked the groceries while the baby slept in its basket. I opened a can of formula, put a pan of water on the stove, and clicked the burner. As I prepared the baby's input, I realized I hadn't checked the diaper for output. I worried what I might find, but the baby hadn't cried, which I figured was a good sign.

But then that became worrisome, too. The baby was asleep when I found it.

It slept through the grocery trip and was still sleeping. I wondered if that was normal, then figured it probably was. Anyway, I didn't have to worry for long.

As I watched the calm little face, the rising and falling chest, the baby woke up. Its eyes popped open, shiny and round, and it watched me with undivided baby-intensity attention. Opened and closed its fists and stuffed them alternately into its toothless mouth. I mixed some formula, following the instructions, while I asked the baby questions and made up answers.

"So, baby, where are you from?"

Staring from the baby.

"Cleveland, you say? And how old are you?"

The baby waved a fist.

"One month? Sorry I misspoke earlier. It won't happen again."

The baby made a sound—not a cry, just a small, exploratory syllable: *inh.*

"Oh, you speak! Maybe you can tell me, then, what's your name?"

The baby smiled.

"You won't say? Well, you're a baby of many secrets."

As I finished mixing the formula, the baby started crying. It was hungry: it drained the bottle without stopping for air, then burped softly and cried again.

"Okay," I said. "Need a change?"

I removed the fleece pants and opened the tabs on its diaper. Wincing, I lifted the flap and saw with surprise that there was no mess. I also saw that the baby was a boy. I lifted his bottom to check for mess underneath, but there was nothing.

"So," I said. "What is it? Still hungry?"

I filled another bottle, and he finished it as fast as the first, then cried again.

"Come on," I said. "You can't still be hungry."

Three more times like that. He gulped a bottle, cried, I filled another, he slugged it down. Remember, I didn't know about babies, so I thought it might be normal.

After five bottles, he stopped crying. Instead he made another baby sound—another *inh*. Reached his tiny hands up to me. Out of nervousness, I hadn't taken him out of the basket other than to check his diaper. But it seemed like he wanted me to hold him, so I picked him up and rested his chest against mine, his little head on my shoulder, and walked laps around my small apartment. I patted his back and hummed, and after a minute he released an enormous belch: a full-grown-man-sized burp that echoed off the bare walls. I held the baby in front of me at arm's length. Spittle ran from one corner of his mouth. He held me in his tractor-beam gaze, not showing any particular emotion, but pure, unwavering attention. Then he cried again.

"You must need changing," I said.

Again I checked the diaper; again it was clean.

"Where'd all that formula go?" I asked. "Where'd you put it?"

He was still crying so I kept troubleshooting. I figured he couldn't be hungry again, so I took him to the window and pointed at things.

"Look," I said. "There's a car—there's a tree—see the woman walking her dog?"

He kept crying. I bounced and rocked him, but it didn't help. I made silly faces. Swung him in the basket, moving it from hand to hand. Walked him around the block. But he just kept crying.

When we got back to the apartment, I was at a loss. Much as I found it hard to imagine, I decided to see if he was hungry. I filled the bottle, and just like before, he slurped it down. Then again with the crying, so again I filled the bottle. It continued like that through the night and into the next morning: He wouldn't sleep, so I didn't sleep. He was alert and observant, even as I got more and more tired. Over and over—he cried, I made formula, and he gulped it down. Every couple hours, I checked the diaper: nothing. He was a perfectly efficient machine, using whatever he took in.

Thursday morning, I called in sick to work to spend the day with my strange little visitor. By midmorning, he had chugged through all the formula I'd bought, so we made another trip to the GroceryPlus. This time I filled the cart with cans of formula.

"You're going to bankrupt me," I said.

The baby stared at me. I pushed the cart to the checkout and started unloading. The cashier, an older woman whose nametag said "Bev," whistled at all the cans.

"Somebody running a home daycare?"

"Oh, ha, yes," I said.

I was thankful for the easy excuse.

"You must have a full house," she said.

She scanned can after can.

"Yup," I said.

I was reluctant to say more—I was worried I'd give myself away.

"Well," she said. "Have fun!"

She held out the receipt.

"Yup," I said.

I pushed the cart all the way back to my apartment, mentally promising to return it later. Inside, I filled a backpack with cans of formula, a bottle, and a thermos of hot water. I packed myself a lunch, picked up the baby in his basket, and headed for the door.

"Come on, Baby," I said. "We're going on a trip."

I'd decided to take the baby to some of my favorite places from when I was a kid. We went to the community garden, the riverfront park, the old town square. All the way, I talked to him, pointing things out, naming them.

"Look at the rabbits! See them crunching on the veggies?"

"Hear the water gurgling? Feel the cool breeze?"

"See the people feeding the birds?"

At each stop, he gulped more formula. At each stop, I thought of times when I was small. When Uncle Jim had taken me to these same places. How much it meant then, how much it still meant to me. At the park, I took out my lunch of a PB&J, chips, and an apple. I hadn't meant to, but I'd packed the same lunch I'd eaten on those outings.

At dusk, after we'd made all our stops, after all the amazing everyday things—colors, animals, elements, events—after consuming between us all the formula, all the sandwiches, and all the hours of the day, we started back toward my apartment. I felt lighter, carrying the baby through the late-summer evening air.

When we got back, the baby cried and I gave him one more bottle. This time, afterward, he didn't cry. Didn't burp. Didn't stare at me, or at the window, or at anything. His eyelids sagged and fluttered, and for the first time since he had woken up more than a day before, he fell sound asleep.

I collapsed on the bed with him sleeping silently in his basket next to me. I'd hardly closed my eyes before I was asleep. I woke up in the pre-dawn to a rustling sound and rolled over.

"What now?" I asked. "Need to eat again? Finally pooped?"

I opened my eyes, then startled and sat up straight. The basket was empty. The next thing I saw was a man, half in shadow, sitting in a chair across the room.

"What's going on?" I said.

"Hey, buddy! It's okay—take it easy," the man said.

The face was obscured, but the voice was familiar.

"Uncle Jim?" I said.

I squinted. He leaned forward out of the shadow and smiled.

"Uncle Jim!" I said.

He grinned even wider.

"How you been?" he asked.

"Shitty," I said, rubbing my eyes and yawning. "Awful. Couldn't believe—you've been there for me forever, and then suddenly you're gone? Like that? I didn't—don't—haven't been able to believe it—haven't been able to think. Then this baby shows up—this baby—wait, where's the baby?"

"Oh, yeah," said Jim. "Hope you don't mind. I borrowed some of your clothes."

He said it like it was an answer to my question.

"What?" I said.

I looked closer and Jim was wearing one of my T-shirts and a pair of my shorts.

"Oh," I said. "That's fine."

I noticed the baby clothes, badly stretched but neatly folded, piled by Jim's feet on the floor. I felt the truth of the situation settle in, followed by its impossibility.

"Hey," said Jim. "I'm hungry. How 'bout breakfast?"

I was still confused. But instead of asking more questions, I swung my legs over the side of the bed and smoothed some of the wrinkles out of my slept-in jeans. I didn't know what to say. But I managed to eke out, "I could eat."

So we both stood up and walked from my bedroom into the Corvair Diner. It was where my kitchen would normally have been. Jim toddled to a booth like he had just relearned how to walk. He sat down and I slid onto the bench across from him. I picked up a ketchup bottle and saltshaker from the table, set them back down. Glanced around the room full of booths and tables and chairs.

"So, then, is this where all the formula went?" I said.

I gestured around us at the cluttered interior of the Corvair, the vinyl and chrome and tile. Jim looked at me in such a way that I knew he wouldn't answer the question. A smiling waitress brought our food on a large, oval tray: two plates of eggs, toast, and bacon; two cups of coffee. She set it down and disappeared. I grinned and reached with my fork to take a bite. But as I reached, the whole diner started to wobble like a plate spun on its edge. And I realized that it really was spinning, with us inside it, and I was dizzy. It teetered, like when the force of the spinner's will starts to wane—when the forces of friction and gravity take over. I wondered about calculations that I couldn't make. About questions to which I had no answers, like: What does it take to sustain a reality that no longer exists? How much willpower—and how much milk powder—would you need to bring the dead to breakfast? And what about lunch or dinner? Can you build a diner out of pure desire? Can you maintain it? What's the overhead like? What would it take?

The wobbling got worse. The plates, glasses, saltshaker, ketchup, napkins, sugar, butter, and jam all slid off the table. Ceramic and glass shattered on impact with the floor and walls. More pliable items bounced and skidded to the corners of the room. I felt hungrier and more tired than I could ever remember. I reached again for my eggs, but they were flattened against the far wall. I spotted my coffee cup emptied on the ceiling. Grasped fruitlessly at a packet of jam that skittered across the floor. And the diner kept spinning, kept tilting at more chaotic angles.

I stopped reaching and looked across at Jim, who grew younger before my eyes. The wrinkles of middle age disappeared. He became, briefly, the twenty-some-year-old man I had first known when I was a baby. Then Jim became a teenager, then a toddler, then an infant. I recognized him clearly as the baby from the basket. Then Jim became an egg—a white oblong orb—which floated, wobbled, and spun off, end over end, into empty space, out through one of the now-disintegrating windows of the diner.

Finally, the walls, floor, and ceiling all split at their seams and drifted in six different directions. The red vinyl booth and gray Formica table fell away. I was left floating, watching the slow, spreading dissipation of a spattery cloud of debris. And I stayed there for a while, quiet and alone, suspended in thick blackness between shimmering points of light.

REGARDING YOUR
MODELING PORTFOLIO

The following letter was mistakenly delivered to my address (#22B) at Odsburg Gardens Apartments, a drab but not unpleasant cluster of low-slung, earth-toned, multi-tenant bungalows that I called home during my time in town.

I opened the letter before I realized it was not intended for me, but for my neighbor Nate Wilkinson (#22A). Before I got around to returning it to him, he moved out and left no forwarding address. I like to think he's off somewhere—I picture Vancouver, BC—working as a successful male model, living his dream. Every time I pass a billboard, I look up to see if Nate (or, more likely, Nate's bare abdomen) is gazing down at me. No sightings so far.

Nate, if you're reading this, I believe in you. Keep chasing your dreams. And don't come after me about this letter. I'm pretty sure, because it was delivered to my address, it is legally mine to do with as I please. It's Americana now. It's an artifact. It's bigger than you or me.

WALLAC

Dear Mr. Wilkinson:

Thank you for your interest in our agency. We at Elite Male Models appreciate having had the chance to review your application materials. I am sorry to inform you that, after much consideration, we do not currently have a position for you on our roster. While your portfolio is impressive—we do not recall ever having seen a photo résumé showcasing such an array of homemade costumes and set pieces—there is one detail we were unable to overlook. Namely: your pectoral muscles are spaced too far apart.

I realize this may seem like a minor or even nitpicky detail. However, please understand: male modeling is an exacting field, and the upscale brands that comprise our client base are exceedingly particular about what/whom they are and are not looking for. Because there are thousands of attractive men out there who dream of being Elite Male Models—who fantasize day in and day out of appearing on billboards and in magazines, in advertisements for underwear, cologne, perfume, blue jeans, cleaning products, lite frozen dinners, etc.—and because these thousands of meticulously sculpted men literally line up around multiple city blocks for a long shot at a major campaign, agencies like ours must be extremely discerning.

Lest there be any confusion or hard feelings, let me be perfectly clear: I am not, in any way, denigrating your physique. You clearly take excellent care of your body through diet and exercise, and Mother Nature evidently gifted you with significant raw materials with which to work. It is simply unfortunate that, through whatever evolutionary or creationist system you believe in, you happen to have pectoral muscles that are spaced just slightly too far apart from one another based on the current commercial aesthetic of an ideal male model.

To put it bluntly, you do not have what we in the industry call "muscle cleavage." Focus group studies have shown that images of men with a visible line of cleavage where their two pectoral muscles abut cause women to respond 11 percent more favorably in verbal assessments of attractiveness and to purchase as much as 14.5 percent more product. This is likely due to aspirational counter-transference of the women's own feelings of inadequacy regarding physical appearance, specifically vis-à-vis analogous breast cleavage. Whatever the reason, the fact remains: muscle cleavage moves product. And if 14.5 percent sounds trivial to you, let me assure you, it is not. Imagine someone told you that you would gain an additional 14.5 percent of overall body fat. Does that sound like a big difference? Of course it does.

Please understand: the reason I have told you exactly what is holding you back from a place on our team is not to make you feel bad about yourself and your inadequately adjacent pectoral muscles. Quite the contrary. I am giving you this feedback so you have a chance, if you so choose, to change your body and, in equal measure, change your fortunes. The only thing standing between you and male modeling success and lucre is the small valley of nothingness between your otherwise perfectly proportional pecs.

With more focused attention on high-intensity resistance exercise targeting the development of the pectorals (specifically the inner pectorals), it might be possible for you to achieve the necessary look. As a rule of thumb, to determine whether you have made it to the desired benchmark, try the following: Place the edge of a sheet of standard copy paper between your pecs and flex them fully. If the sheet of paper remains in place, suspended in your muscle cleavage, you have achieved the optimal adjacency. If not, keep working at it, and try not to feel discouraged.

Please note that the above paragraphs are in no way meant to be construed as a conditional guarantee of employment. However, if you do manage to find an exercise or set of exercises (dumbbell flys, for example) of which you could perhaps do several dozen extra sets per week and thereby achieve a more satisfactory abutment of your pectoralis majori, or, if you were to elect surgical pectoral enhancement, which we are in no way endorsing, but which is certainly a possibility if you were to decide that it is the right choice for you, then we would be happy to reopen your application and review your updated/augmented portfolio.

Thank you again for your interest, and best of luck in your future endeavors.

Sincerely,
Vance Mandlebaum
Talent Liaison
Elite Male Models, LLC

IN MEMORIAM

I transcribed the following from audio recorded during one of many evenings spent at Anderson's Tavern. The impromptu memorial service took place among the regular patrons who happened to be there, which seemed fitting—as in death, so in life, or what have you. The speaker, a generously tattooed and pierced man in his twenties wearing a black T-shirt, black baseball cap, and torn jeans, rapped his knuckles on the zinc bar top, cleared his throat, and began.

To wit, I was offered—and accepted—one of the token packages of cigarettes mentioned below. Seeing as I do not smoke tobacco, or at least not industrial cigarettes, I still have them in a drawer of my desk as a memento of the occasion and the serendipity that placed me there to witness it.

A'right so this's a story 'bout my uncle Mikey, on account o' whose memory we're here today, here at Anderson's Tavern which y'know was 'is favorite place, I remember this one time it must'a been what three, four years ago now me an' Mikey walk in here an' Cal the bartender—wave t' everybody Cal— Cal says, "Hey Big Mikey," 'cause Mikey was in here all the time an' him an' Cal was friends, Cal even loaned Mikey some money once an' I 'member they come to blows over it but no bad blood, it's water under the bridge, an' so Cal says, "The usual?" an' Mikey nods an' heaves hisself belly-first up on the stool an' Cal slaps down a paper coaster an' thunks down a twenty-two ounce o' Bud Heavy which y'know was Mikey's drink an' Mikey says "Bottoms up" or "Five o'clock some-where" or "Nectar o' the gods" or, no, it was early—'bout ten thirty in the mornin' 'cause I remember we'd been standin' out waitin' for Cal t'unlock the front door an' gettin' stares from people goin' to the diner for breakfas' or Stardust for coffee an' Mikey's feelin' embarrassed, 'cause what's it say 'bout him, waitin' to get in for the first beer o' the day before noon, nursin' a hangover or let's face it a drunkover, so Mikey says "Breakfast o' champions" to sorta make it seem okay, sorta poke fun like if you can joke 'bout it then it's not a problem, right, an' he forces a laugh but the laugh turns into a nasty cough 'cause y'know Mikey was a heavy smoker—he loved his Marbs—an' probably should'a quit or least got checked out by a doctor but he didn't have insurance an' doctors ain't cheap, besides there's other things come first out his paycheck like his beers an' smokes, so anyways Mikey's hackin' somethin' fierce but he just picks up a cocktail napkin off the bar an' wipes the black phlegm out his mustache an' stuffs the napkin in his jeans pocket an' that's that—no drama—'cause Mikey was no-nonsense, y'know, he wore his troubles on the inside, kept it close to his chest, an' so Cal turns to me an' says, "What'll it be young'un," so I'm like "You guys got Dew?" 'cause 'course I wasn't old enough to drink then an' Cal's like, "Nah, Coke products," so I'm like, "A'right just gimme a lemonade," an' Cal nods to me an' then turns an' starts chattin' up these two waitresses who're a'right lookin' but look like they're in high school or maybe nineteen at the most so you got to figure somewhere in that barely-legal-if-they're-legal-at-all range an' Cal's, what, forty, forty-five an' balding an' got sweat stains in the pits of his polo which is tight but not where he'd like, meanin' he's maybe five-nine an' two-sixty an' not muscly, no offense Cal, just sayin', an' so I'm thinkin' *c'mon Cal they could be your daughters for chrissakes* an' just as I'm thinkin' 'bout sayin' somethin', Cal turns back 'round to us an' he's like, "Yo Mikey, how 'bout I get you some wings or some nachos, you ought to eat somethin'," 'cause he knows if Mikey don't get some food in him he'll be hurtin' after his second twenty-two in twenty minutes an' Cal's gotta decide now: does he stop servin' Mikey an' get on the receivin' end o' some misplaced temper or keep servin' him an' hope to god Mikey don't make a scene 'cause y'know Mikey'd make a scene if he got riled an' o' course Mikey's too full from the beer an' y'know he had his stomach troubles an' so he won't even touch the free peanuts let alone some hot wings, so I figure if he ain't eatin' I will, so I say to Cal, "I'll take some o' them nachos," an' so now the two waitresses are standin' by the end o' the bar poppin' their gum an' the lunch crowd isn't in yet so what else they got to do besides shoot the shit, an' one of 'em's lookin' our way, she's lookin' at Mikey specifically, an' I can hear her sayin', "Oh god, Madisyn, look at this guy, that's so sad, I hope I'm never like that, or worse yet my boyfriend, please just kill me, you know I think maybe Tamryn might be an alcoholic, did you see how drunk she got at Devin's party last weekend, but then again maybe she just likes to party, right, like it's just a thing to do, right, but then I start wondering am I partying too much, am I headed down a slippery slope, should I be getting an internship or something," an' the other one just shrugs an' glances at her phone an' I'm thinkin' *shit I hope Mikey's not listenin' to 'em* but I can tell he's not, an' besides he's all flushed in the face now an' you can see he's feelin' right with the world an' even if he heard 'em he wouldn't be bothered, he'd probably just laugh it off an' so now Mikey says, "Yo Cal, gimme another," an' Cal's like, "Maybe you need to cool it Mikey," an' Mikey's like, "The only thing needs to be cool's the beer in the fuckin' mug Cal-vin," he kinda shouts an' slurs an' stands up an' starts wobblin' 'round swayin' an' I'm thinkin' *shit what-all's gonna happen now* an' Mikey's turnin' green like he might puke an' holdin' the bar rail to keep steady an' after maybe ten seconds Mikey stops swayin' an' looks real serious an' says real low-an'-slow, "I said gimme another beer Cal don't make me slap you," an' Cal's eyes go real wide an' I'm thinkin' *ah shit here goes,* but then Cal cracks up an' next Mikey's laughin' too god rest his soul an' then he's wet-hackin' tar an' whatnot in his phlegm-napkin an' the two waitresses are lookin' like their eyes're 'bout to bug out their heads but you can tell they're tryin' to keep from laughin' too an' the tension just goes right out the room an' Cal thunks down another beer an' another lemonade an' he's like, "You're a real sonofabitch Mikey y'know," an' I suppose that's my point, Mikey always knew how to lighten the mood, right up to the end, when his lungs an' liver an' pancreas was all givin' out he never did complain, least not that I heard, just livin' his life, an' you'd've never known he was dyin', that's for sure, least not from his demeanor, though maybe from his coughin' blood an' phlegm an' from his faintin' spells an' from his gray complexion an' the way he didn't hardly know who or where he was 'round the end there, but he always tried hard to lift the spirits o' everybody 'round him, an' that's somethin' to be said for him that you can't say 'bout everybody, so R-I-goddamn-P Mikey, you lived 'til you died an' it is what it is an' we're all better off for knowin' you—oh, an' don't forget we're sendin' 'round Bud Heavies for everybody compliments o' the family an' also help yourselfs to a pack o' Mikey's Marbs 'cause he'd just stocked up on a couple o' cartons right 'fore he passed, but isn't that just the way it goes, an' you can't take it with you, so let's don't let 'em go to waste.

SITTER'S NOTES

The following is a reproduction of a handwritten note, jotted across several lined legal pad pages, which I found tucked inside a horticultural guidebook that I purchased at the Odsburg Public Library book sale. As a bibliophile, I can never resist a good book sale. And as a socio-anthropo-lingui-lore-ologist, such sales are true treasure troves of lost and forgotten ephemera and personal artifacts. If you want to be sure to lose track of a piece of paper, there's nothing better than to fold it into the pages of a book.

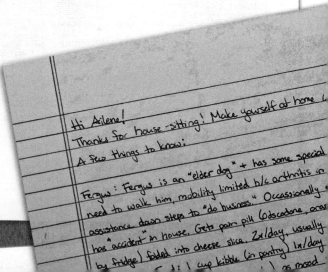

Hi Arlene!
Thanks for house-sitting! Make yourself at home —
A few things to know:

Fergus: Fergus is an "elder dog" + has some special
need to walk him, mobility limited b/c arthritis in
assistance down steps to "do business." Occasionally
has "accident" in house. Gets pain pill (oxycodone, or an
by fridge) folded into cheese slice. 2x/day, usually
1 cup kibble (in pantry) 1x/day
as mood

Hi Ailene!

Thanks for house-sitting! Make yourself at home while here.
A few things to know:

Fergus: Fergus is an "elder dog" & has some special needs.
Won't need to walk him, mobility limited b/c arthritis in hips.
May need assistance down steps to "do business." Occasionally
doesn't make it & has "accident" in house. Gets pain pill
(Odscodone, orange bottle in cabinet by fridge) folded into
cheese slice, 2×/day, usually midmorning & before bed. Food:
1 cup kibble (in pantry) 1×/day & we spoil him so he gets bacon
treats (also in pantry) as mood strikes &/or when he wheedles.

Delia: Delia is an indoor cat. She ~~may try~~ will try to get outside. DO NOT let out as she ~~may not~~ will not find way back.
Has very poor sense of direction, balance, etc., due to damaged
cochlea from ear infection when she was a kitten. Also do
not push her off counter/tabletop/etc. Same reason. Let her
go where she pleases, EXCEPT OUTSIDE. Also has vertigo
& takes vertigo meds (Odsvertis, 1 pill 1×/day—yellow bottle,
cabinet by fridge) w/ spoonful of salmon paste (can in fridge).
Food: ½ cup dry in a.m., ½ cup wet in p.m. Scoop litter box
(1st floor half-bath, litter bags under sink) 1×/day.

Hubert: Hubert is a zebra angelfish. Mostly self-sufficient. Tank has filter, etc., no need to clean. We will clean when we get back. DO NOT try to clean. Food: 1 generous sprinkle (can on top of tank) 1×/day. Also gets ½ pill Odslexa (green bottle, cabinet by fridge) for anxiety, crushed and sprinkled into tank 1×/day.

Renoir: Prickly pear cactus. Needs nothing. We will water before leaving; only gets water 1× every 3 wks. Do not water. Overwatering will kill him. DO NOT WATER.

Pluto: Pluto is the ficus. Needs constant, moderate moisture. Comes from damp environ. Spritz soil & leaves w/ spray bottle (on floor by pot) 2-4×/day. Play some music 1×/day. Not too particular what kind, but best if it has violins.

Celine: Our house ghost. You may/may not believe in ghosts. OK either way. We call "Celine" b/c feels like feminine energy. Mostly creaks floorboards on porch & rocks rocking chair. Seems harmless. We light candle most nights, burn sage— seems to calm/soothe. You may do same, or not. Your choice. Interesting to see what happens.

Thanks again so much! Enjoy anything in fridge/pantry & see you in a few days!

THE RABBIT AFTER THE DOG

The following story of canine-to-rabbit reincarnation was trans-mitted to me telepathically by a rabbit after I fed it a carrot outside the Odsburg Community Garden. The story was not transmitted in words, but rather as a single mental impression, so I took the necessary and practical liberty (for your sake, Dear Reader) of translating it into words. Believe it or don't, but that's what happened.

Full disclosure: I was taking prescription painkillers at the time. Long story short, I had just had an impacted tooth extracted, and the dentist wrote me a script for Odscodone. Or maybe it was Odsmorphone. But it doesn't matter. I know what I experienced. The vision was vivid as daylight.

The rabbit was small, brown, fuzzy, and adorable, with one of those little white cottontails, like in a children's picture book.

I fell asleep lying on my side, tongue lolling across my plush, spongy bed. As I slipped into unconsciousness, the pain in my hips, shoulders, and legs—the persistent aching that stretched down into the pads of my paws—grew dim. The pain had gotten sharper lately when I tried to run. After a few steps, I would feel it radiating down my spine, and it would bring me, whining and sniffling, to a halt. The feeling was less intense for a while after I ate one of the salty treats I'd been getting so many of, but it never went away completely—only grew more or less intense, causing me to wince and whimper more or less, making me more tired or slightly less. But tonight, as I fell asleep, I was more tired than I could ever remember. I slumped into my soft cushion and drifted amid the dull pain quickly into sleep.

I woke in darkness, lying on my stomach in soft dirt. I felt the wind blowing cool on my wet nose but couldn't hear it nor pick up any scent. My eyes adjusted to the soft glow of moonlight. High on the horizon, along a ridge, I saw the silhouettes of two tall, leafy trees and the shadow of a figure, about my size, moving between them. Directly in front of me, a few dozen strides ahead, were many neat rows of tall, green stalks. They swayed silently, their silky tassels ruffled in the inaudible, unscented breeze. I stood up gingerly and my joints, though slow-moving, felt surprisingly free of pain. I stretched my shoulders, nose to the ground, front paws pressed into the earth.

A mottled brown rabbit bounded past me out of the darkness, right in front of my nose. I followed it instinctively, keeping it in sight, closing at its heels. As I ran, my paws flipped clods of loamy dirt behind me. The rabbit led me in scrabbling arcs, weaving smooth S-curves across the expanse of unfenced land and into the cornfield. I tracked it by sight—not my strongest sense, but it was all I had. I still couldn't find the rabbit's scent, nor any other.

Even though I was running as fast as I could, the rabbit gained ground, widening the swath of land between its body and mine. It approached the wall of corn, threatening to disappear within the green lattice. I felt no fatigue, but knew that I was too slow to catch the rabbit unless it faltered or flagged. My legs felt sluggish, like running through thick beef gravy.

I lost sight of the rabbit—I blinked and it was gone. Now there were just its small footprints in the soil, still fresh. I followed their curves, back and forth, zigzagging across the field. I hoped to spot their maker around the next turn, down the next furrow, between the green rows of stalks. My legs, still soupy, didn't seem to touch the ground but still carried me onward. Then the leaves were slapping at my nose, at my ears, as my body plunged into the field of green pillars.

Finally even the rabbit's footprints disappeared amid the thicket of stalks. I was left with nothing to track—no scent, no sight, no trail. I felt the fatigue of the chase in my slow-motion legs. I stopped and sniffed and still smelled nothing. I pawed the ground; I tried to howl but made no sound. I turned some small, slow circles and laid my body in the dirt.

Nearing sleep, I sensed something drawing close. It rustled the stalks and bent them outward in a wide V around its body, casting shadows in the moonlight. In a small clearing in front of me, from between the rows of stalks, the rabbit reappeared.

It was much larger now—many times my size. As big as a bear I once encountered in the woods. The rabbit was dragging a thick blanket—a blanket woven of darkness deeper and thicker than the surrounding night. Stepping slowly, heavily, it approached and then moved past me, dragging its blanket over my head, blocking the wafer of moon and sealing me in a velvety-soft, seamless pitch-blackness, warm like a womb.

After what seemed like a long time, the blanket of darkness slipped away. I was pink and soft and slippery and suckling for white warm milk. A faded past lingered, dreamlike. But even in the slurred and blurry presence of its echo, I felt new potential. My tail, which had so recently wagged, twitched tightly. My ears no longer flopped, but stood oblong, scanning for threats—tuned to the movements and rustlings of invisible predators. My nose still itched to scratch the scent from the wind—not to track and hunt, but to elude. My joints and muscles no longer twinged with arthritis and fatigue; they throbbed and yearned to spring and spring and spring. My hunger, when it wanted more than milk, would not be for beef or bones, rawhide or rubber, but for lettuce, beans, and carrots. Fibrous, vegetal things. When the safety of my soft mother slipped away, I would be ready to forage, poised for flight. All of me—muscles, eyes, ears, nose, even bones—flitted quickly, ticked at a higher tempo. I felt deep, abiding love for grasses and the desire to be—as I once had been, and as I dimly knew in that moment I was—under the soft, loamy earth. In the warmth of a warren, burrowed.

MUNICIPAL MINUTIAE

The following is a copy of the minutes from a recent meeting of the Odsburg Town Council. They are a matter of public record, available to any interested party. I felt they might lend some perspective on local color, the general flavor of town business. I procured them, as any interested citizen could, by visiting the Office of the Town Clerk. The office was cramped, trimmed with faux-wood paneling and lined with bulging, dust-covered binders. It smelled like a pine tree air freshener.

The clerk's nameplate said "Carl Ortman." I would place his age somewhere in the neighborhood of forty, and he had an air, rather like the office, of rumpled organization. When he looked up from his computer to greet me, he adjusted his glasses, as if he might be sussing out my solidity as I came properly into focus. I suppose the clerk's office doesn't get many visitors.

He asked me which meeting I wanted the minutes from, and I told him any recent meeting would do just fine. "Surprise me," I think I said. He frowned, but complied.

Town of Odsburg
Monthly town council meeting minutes

Location: Odsburg Public Library, Meeting Room 1

Attendees:
Council Chair: Martin Longacre
Councilmembers: Ken Cherwith, Bill Davis,
   KellyLyn Hawkins
Town Administrator: Lillian Vance
Legal Counsel: Lewis Nordquist, Esq.
Residents: Carmichael Jones, Carmichelle Jones,
   Lou Herman, Gus Lawrence

Call to order: Meeting is called to order at 7:04 p.m. by
Chairman Longacre, followed by Pledge of Allegiance and
moment of silence in honor of our troops. Vote to ratify minutes of previous meeting passes 4–0.

First order of business: Proposal to allow licensing for a
MightyMax Mini Mart to open within town limits. Councilman
Cherwith raises concern that this could hurt locally owned
Gas-n-Go convenience store, possibly put it out of business.
Mr. Herman suggests it may also put Odsburg Five and Dime

out of business. Mr. Lawrence tells Mr. Herman that Odsburg Five and Dime has been out of business for decades, calls Mr. Herman "old coot." Mr. Herman says yes, he remembers that, but notwithstanding the store's closure, might it not be disrespectful to the memory of Odsburg Five and Dime to allow a national chain such as MightyMax. Councilman Cherwith reiterates the value of local business, both in general and specifically with respect to still-existing businesses, namely the Gas-n-Go. Councilwoman Hawkins concurs. Councilman Cherwith concedes, however, that he enjoys MightyMax Super Slushees and it would be nice to not have to drive to Klester to get one. Chairman Longacre and Councilman Davis concur. Vote to allow licensing of MightyMax Mini Mart passes 3–1.

Second order of business: Proposal to reinstate long-standing but recently discontinued Odsburg Cherry Festival. Chairman Longacre recalls many fond memories of Cherry Festival— various contests of cherry-eating, pit-spitting, cobbler-making, pie-baking, tree-chopping, lie-telling, etc.—but cannot overlook the fact that funding is not there; asks where funding would come from. Councilwoman Hawkins suggests a fundraiser. Councilman Cherwith asks what kind of fundraiser could raise that kind of funds. Councilwoman Hawkins asks what kind of funds are needed, since she is new to council and only joined post-cessation of Cherry Festival, hence does not have a sense of the budget. Councilman Cherwith wonders if the council could request funds from OdsWellMore, seeing as they have helped with such things in the past. Could they sponsor in exchange for advertising, PR, so forth. Councilman Davis says OdsWellMore might attempt to co-opt, as has been known to happen, vis-à-vis things they supply funding for, such as former annual Odsburg Pet Parade, now OdsWellMore

PetMeds Pet-athlon and Clinic Featuring OdsFleaFree and OdsWormGard. Mr. Nordquist, Esq., clears throat, scribbles on legal pad. Chairman Longacre suggests council be careful with criticisms of generous folks at OdsWellMore. Vote to table conversation until later date passes 4–0.

Third order of business: Proposal to rezone and convert vacant lot where Corvair Diner used to be into public park and playground. Councilwoman Hawkins says, as parent of two young children, she would love to see project approved and completed. Chairman Longacre asks again about funding. Councilman Cherwith and Councilman Davis make sounds of concurrence. Mr. and Mrs. Jones offer that they have begun organizing a group of concerned parents who will provide manual labor, assist with planning and organizing, and conduct fundraisers to support project. Chairman Longacre asks, if council were to approve rezoning, would parents' group take lead on the project so as to remove burden from council, which already has a full docket. Mr. and Mrs. Jones answer in affirmative. Chairman Longacre shrugs, as do Councilman Davis and Councilman Cherwith. Councilwoman Hawkins gives Mr. and Mrs. Jones thumbs-up. Vote to rezone former Corvair lot for park/public use, no town funds allocated, passes 4–0.

Fourth order of business: Request for closed session. Mr. Nordquist, Esq., requests closed session with council to discuss matter of importance. Councilwoman Hawkins asks for what purpose. Mr. Nordquist declines to elaborate, restates request for closed session. Councilwoman Hawkins acknowledges her relative newness, but wonders whether all public business should be handled publicly, for sake of accountability. Vote to meet with Mr. Nordquist, Esq., in closed session passes 3–1.

Fifth order of business: Councilman Davis makes motion to adjourn public meeting. Motion passes 4–0. Meeting is adjourned at 8:01 p.m. Councilman Cherwith makes motion to reconvene immediately after in closed session with Mr. Nordquist, Esq. Motion passes 4–0, though unclear whether Councilwoman Hawkins was voting in affirmative or raising another question regarding closed meeting. Notes from closed meeting to be filed separately, not subject to public review.

Respectfully recorded,
Lillian Vance, Town Administrator

KENNY CAN-DO

The following is transcribed from a field recording. I made the recording while crouching behind a conveniently parked car outside the dining room entrance of the Goose & Gander Grill. Known by many in town as the place to go for a "nice meal," the Goose & Gander is a frequent destination for birthdays, anniversaries, and dates.

I was early for a dinner engagement I had scheduled for later in the evening, and I never miss an opportunity to collect a good recording. I got an oil stain on the knee of my chinos and scuffed one of my shoes in the process, but I consider that a small price to pay in service of my work.

The speaker was a short, athletically built man in a sport coat, jeans, and loafers. He appeared to be in his mid-thirties, had a bit of a bald spot, and was graying around the temples. I gathered from context that his name was Kenny. I did not see him inside the restaurant, but I like to think he gathered his courage and went on his date, and that it went well.

Okay, Kenny, you can do this. No big deal, right? It's just a blind date, right? What's the worst that could happen?

Wait. What if I have something in my teeth? Lettuce? Did I eat lettuce earlier? Or parsley? When was the last time I ate parsley? Tabbouleh at the Turkish place? How long can parsley stay in your teeth? Did I floss last night? Do I floss enough in general? What if I have bad breath? What if I spit on her when I say hello? Or what if I blurt out something really thoughtless? Like, "That dress is unflattering on you." Or, "That doesn't look like your natural hair color." Or, "You're wearing a lot of makeup. Were you up late last night? On another date?"

What if she actually was on another date last night? What if the guy was richer, taller, younger, and more muscular than me? What if he had a better paying, more exciting job? What if he was a professional skydiver or a Fortune 500 CFO? Or both? Are those necessarily more appealing than an assistant regional sales manager? What if she just wants security and stability—then do I come out on top? In that case, will she think my Mustang is too dangerous? Should I go trade it in real quick for a Focus?

What if she's into big guys? What if she thinks I'm not fat enough? Can I call this a paunch, or is it more of a mini-gut? What if she was on a date with a woman last night and she decided she likes women better? What if we really hit it off but she tells me it won't work because she's not into men anymore?

Or what if she's married and has kids and she's doing this on a whim? Just for a kick, while her husband thinks she's visiting her sister in Steilacoom? What if that sister is single and cute? Will she maybe give me her sister's number?

What if she doesn't like that I'm a single dad? Should I have told her that before I asked her out? What if she's okay with me being a single dad but hates my kid? Is Dewey likeable? Is he hateable? Can I judge his likeability or hateability, or am I too close to the situation? Should I ask his teacher?

What if all this is for nothing? Am I wasting my time worrying about it?

What if she stands me up? Should I preemptively stand her up to take the upper hand? What if I stand her up and she doesn't stand me up? Am I prepared to deal with the consequences of looking like a jerk just to cultivate a false sense of power? Would she give me another chance after something like that? Would she maybe be even more attracted to me? Do some women really like jerks? Could I be happy with a woman who likes jerks? Would I end up letting her down when she finds out I'm pretty nice?

What if I trip over my shoelace on my way in and nosedive on the sidewalk? What if I break my nose and there's blood everywhere? What if she has to call 911—or rush me to the hospital herself? What if I bleed all over her car? What if she leaves me there bleeding all over myself instead and tells me she's sorry, but she just got new upholstery?

Is this an okay place for a first date? Should I have suggested someplace more casual? "Casualer"? Someplace without tablecloths? Will she think I'm pretentious? Will she think I'm richer than I really am? What if there's nothing here she can eat? What if she's allergic to gluten? And soy? And corn? And nuts? And shellfish? And water?

Should I be myself? Let it all hang out? Or be on my best behavior? Try to make a good first impression? An impression that will fade over time—that will corrode and reveal my true personality—because nobody can keep up an act forever? What if I keep it up 'til we're married, and then, when I let my guard down, she hates the real me? What if she does the same and I hate the real her too and then we're miserable together? What if we have kids by then? What if we have to make a terrible choice: a messy divorce that scars our kids or a long, unhappy life in a loveless marriage?

Or what if we love each other but hate our kids? What if our kids get the worst of both our qualities? What if they get my temper, laziness, and eczema, and her … what might her bad qualities be? What if her bad qualities aren't as bad? Will I feel inadequate in comparison? What if her worst qualities are chewing loudly and murdering cats?

What if we fall in love, marry, have kids, and then find out we're long-lost half-siblings? Would the marriage be annulled? Would we go on living together? Even though we know society forbids our unholy union? Would it be too weird? What if we're just cousins?

Was this even the place we agreed on? Am I remembering wrong? How will I know who she is? What if I meet another woman instead? Another woman who's also here for a blind date and has the same name as the woman I'm supposed to meet? And she was supposed to meet a different man with the same name as me? What if we never recognize the mistake and we go on for the rest of our lives having met the wrong people? But we turn out to be the right people for each other after all, and we and the other mismatched couple both find true love? And we live happily until death, in old age, from natural causes—the end? Wouldn't that make a good story?

Could she be here already? Will she be at the bar? Or will she have gotten a table? What does it say about her if she's at the bar? And if she got a table should I demand a different table? To show her who the man is? *Who the man is?* Did I really just say that?

What if I go in and get a table and she's sitting at the bar and we spend the whole evening waiting for each other? Each thinking we've been stood up, like a scene from a romantic comedy? What if I'm living inside a real-life romantic comedy? What if I'm on a reality TV show and I don't know it until after the date is over? Would I sign the release and let them air it? Would I be paid? How much? If it went well, would I agree to a second date, even if it was staged? Could I trust this woman if she set me up on TV? What if she doesn't know about it, either? What if we're the only ones not in on it, and all our family and friends are sitting in a back room of the restaurant watching us on hidden camera? Would I ever be able to trust anyone again?

Wait, is that her? Could that be her over there? Is she looking at me, or looking past me at someone else? Someone better dressed or with whiter teeth? Is she coming this way? Do I really want to do this? Do I have any choice at this point?

What're the odds this is going to go well? One in ten? One in a hundred? Is that an engagement ring? Which hand is that? What do I lead with? How do I introduce myself? "Hi, I'm Kenny"? Is "Kenny" too childish? Should I say "Ken"? "Kenneth"? "I'm Ken, I'll be your blind date this evening ..."? "Hello, I'm Kenneth, and you must be—"?

Oh no, what's her name? Sara? Cheryl? Saryl? That's not a name, is it? Can I just mumble something indistinct? "Hi, you must be Shamumblemumble—"? And what does she do for work? Don't I already know this? Is it rude not to remember?

Does she look like my type? Do I have a type? What is it? Curvy brunette? Slender blonde? Buxom redhead? What if she's not my type and I don't know it, because I don't know what my type is? Can what I don't know really not hurt me? What am I so afraid of? How bad could this be? What have I got to lose? Do I really want to answer that question?

Okay, okay, it's definitely her. Okay, Kenny, you can do this.

SOUVENIRS

The following is transcribed from a field recording. It was told to me by Heidi Derwitz, thirty-two—appearance: curvy, shoulder-length red hair, 5′6″; profession: reference librarian; likes: small dogs, white wine, and classic novels—during a dinner date at the Goose & Gander. Heidi had chicken cordon bleu; I had prime rib. The atmosphere of the place was charming and palpably romantic: white tablecloths, candles, and fresh flowers on the table.

I had met Heidi at Go-Around-Again, the secondhand store. She was dropping off several large boxes of items for consignment when I stopped in looking for a blanket, I believe, or perhaps for some other odd or end—I can't say I remember my precise purpose that day. As I've said, my trips to the store were not infrequent. At any rate, Heidi and I struck up a conversation and she gave me her number.

It did not develop into a romantic relationship, in case you are wondering, but we remained friendly. I would see her from time to time in the stacks or behind the desk of the Odsburg Public Library and would wave or say hello. She almost always appeared to be daydreaming, and looked as if she were balancing an unwieldy load.

It started with a few knickknacks:

A tiny model pickaxe embossed with the words *Yukon Territory*. A statuette of a brown bear standing on its hind legs, brandishing the California flag. A ceramic teacup-sized covered wagon that reads *Oregon Trail: Westward Ho!*

I noticed them all one day on a bookshelf in my bedroom, and I assumed my mother must have sent them, mementos from her post-retirement pilgrimages. Trips I had heard about during rambling phone conversations while I did my hair and makeup and got ready for work, or sat and ate a quick micro-waved dinner with a half-glass of wine, checking my email while she prattled on.

I thought, in the perpetually busy and distracted bustling of days—between bad dates, long hours at the office, and endless trips to conferences—I must have opened packages containing these objects, set them out on display, and then promptly forgotten about them, only to find them again later, as though for the first time.

Like I said, it started with knickknacks—easy enough things to misplace or forget about or receive without even registering.

But then, a while later, there was an end table.

It was one of those side-table-and-floor-lamp-in-one deals that looked straight from the seventies, with a gilt-edged glass top, four lathe-turned wooden legs, and a hunter green lampshade.

If I didn't know any better, I'd think it might have lived in my grandparents' house when I was growing up—the sort of thing that one of my cousins would have smashed his forehead against as a toddler. If he went seeking consolation, he'd have been chastised by some cigarette-wielding, liquor-swirling great-aunt. I can almost hear the rasping, "That's what you get for running in the house!"

But how did it end up here—in my apartment?

No idea.

Next was a guitar.

To be clear, I don't play the guitar. I don't play anything. I have no desire to learn, no particular ear for music. I have no *reason* to have acquired a guitar. I had a boyfriend once who played, but I can't imagine he'd have left it here, all this time, unnoticed until now.

It's an old acoustic model, that much I know. Rich, honey-colored wood, half-lacking its lacquer, covered all over with fine, crosshatched scratches. It has worn-down swirls of mother-of-pearl along the neck, and a warm, musty smell inside. When I plucked at the corroded, coppery strings, they gave a satisfying, rattly twang.

But, of course, that's not my point. My point is: what is it doing in my apartment? I broke up with it—I mean, with the guy who must have left it here—a long time ago.

The list goes on—those are just some highlights.

The more I've looked, the more I've found my apartment is full of things that I can't remember picking out: cooking utensils, bath towels, old clothes, plastic toys, framed photos, scented candles, paperback and hardcover books. Things I'm sure I never bought, that I don't recall receiving, but that somehow made their way into my already-tiny living space, making it impossibly smaller.

It wasn't such an issue at first. But lately I can hardly sit down or walk from bedroom to bathroom without climbing over piles or shoving things out of the way.

The latest arrival is an armoire.

That's right: an armoire.

How exactly one of those arrives unannounced, I couldn't begin to guess, but I woke up on Sunday to find it blocking half the doorway to the kitchen. I stubbed three toes on it stumbling through to make coffee. When I pulled open its doors, an avalanche of mothballed business suits, faded military uniforms, grass-stained overalls, and a whole slew of cable-knit wool cardigans nearly knocked me over. Gold buttons and hooks on the plackets and lapels winked up at me in the slanting mid-morning light, like we shared some obscure half-secret.

I think the armoire is made of cherry wood. It's beautiful, really. But despite its charm, it's maybe not so practical for the space; it takes up a full third of the living room, so I've had to push the couch into the corner.

Then again, whether I want it or not, I have no idea how I'd ever get it out of there. It would never fit through the front door—at least not in one piece.

All else being equal, and other concerns aside, I do have to say it goes nicely with the antique sideboard that showed up yesterday, big as a coffin, covered with huge, dust-grayed doilies. The sideboard's wide drawers are packed full of tarnished, hand-monogrammed flatware, delicate gold leaf peeling from the engraved letters—three initials that, though I can't quite place them, feel vaguely, distantly familiar.

TESTAMENT

The following is a reproduction of a document—yellow carbon copy paper, from an original typed on a typewriter—entrusted to me by Gus Lawrence, ninety, of 304 Front Street. Gus told me many times, over cups of black coffee on his front porch, that he was enmeshed in a public and longstanding feud with his neighbor Lou Herman, eighty-nine, of 306 Front Street. Neither Gus nor Lou would elaborate on the origin of the feud. Their mutual friend Mel Hines seemed to have something to do with it, but sadly Mel was not lucid enough to elucidate. Perhaps it goes without saying that each of the two men insisted that he was in the right and held the moral high ground. When I mentioned Gus's document to Lou, he scoffed audibly and said, "Wills are bullshit. And I'm gonna live forever."

Upon the occasion of my death, be it known that I, Gus Lawrence, wish for my belongings to be disposed of by way of a public auction, to be held in the old town square on Main Street, across from the Thirsty Dachshund. And be it known that I wish also for my home, at 304 Front Street, to be sold at auction, with said auction to be conducted silently using nautical semaphore flags.

Be it further known that, with my wife of forty years having predeceased me, and with my two sons having effectively disowned me, having moved to Albany and Albuquerque, respectively, and never calling, I wish that all proceeds of said auction, along with other monies comprising my estate, after deducting necessary expenses for my cremation, memorial, and other arrangements detailed below, should be bequeathed and conveyed to the Trumbull County SPCA for the purpose of rescuing and rehabilitating stray and abused dogs, cats, rabbits, reptiles, and other domestic animals, with the exception of guinea pigs. I do not like guinea pigs.

Be it additionally known that, for the occasion of my memorial, I wish for my body to be cremated and for my cremated remains to be disposed of in the following manner: they shall be dispensed into a piñata, preferably in the shape of a horse, though exceptions may be made as needed based on availability; the piñata shall be suspended from a lamppost on the footbridge over the Sillagumquit River; and whosoever attends the memorial shall be invited to take turns striking at the piñata with a dowel, broom handle, or other such stick, until the piñata breaks apart, spilling my cremated remains into the peacefully flowing river; whereupon a twenty-one gun salute shall commence, and all in attendance shall gaze on my ashes as they float, sink, or flow down the river, around the bend, and out of sight.

Moreover, be it known that, after the dispensation of my remains, I wish for my memorial to continue with dinner or hors d'oeuvres in the banquet room at the Goose & Gander, with food to be served to all who should attend, and that it should be something good, fancy but not too fancy, such as prime rib if it shall be a sit-down dinner, or stuffed mushrooms and spinach puffs if it shall be something more stand-uppy and informal. Afterward, I wish for there to be a festive gathering at my house (this shall be a condition of the aforementioned house auction, that the memorial shall be allowed to take place there), wherein everyone will wear a paper mask of my face (portrait photo to be attached for this purpose) and will, for the duration of the party, address one another as "Gus" and say the sorts of things that I always used to say. At the party, black coffee and whiskey will be served—something pretty good, but not too pricey, as I do not want all my money going to get other people drunk on expensive booze.

Be it known, too, that if the occasion of my death should be deemed suspicious, I wish for an investigation to occur, and if the police should be deemed to be doing an insufficient job in terms of competence or in terms of zeal and vigor, I wish for a private detective to be hired, again using funds as necessary from my estate, to investigate any and all suspicious circumstances, persons, events, objects, and so forth, and let such investigation begin with my rival and sworn enemy Lou Herman if he should survive me, and with his heirs and assigns should he predecease me, for I would not put it past him to issue some form of decree or order, by way of his own last will and testament, that he should want me killed or at least wish to have my life, livelihood, and well-being interfered with, and that he, being a slippery son-of-a-you-know-what, should perhaps even go so far as to condition the dispensation of his own estate on the performance of some such act or acts to intervene in my health and/or aliveness.

Be it lastly known, and so stated by any and all who should witness it, that this, my last will and testament, is superior in every measurable respect, objectively and subjectively speaking, to the last will and testament of my sworn rival and enemy Lou Herman, whatsoever the form or contents of his last will and testament might be.

SUNDAY LUNCH

I witnessed the following events while peering in through one of several first-floor windows of a small, well-kept Craftsman on Front Street. In my defense, all the windows were wide open, so it was rather like the events below were taking place in public. As luck would have it, the couple never seemed to notice me, which at the time led me to wonder whether I might have spent so much time working at blending in that I had actually become invisible. Of course, in hindsight, I imagine I would have been outed had they only happened to look in my direction.

I should also note that, prior to the events described below, I gathered and ate some mushrooms of an unconfirmed variety— earthy and a little bit nutty in flavor—from a flowerbox beneath the window where I stood. It is entirely possible that the consumption of those mushrooms may have had an effect on the nature and quality of my subsequent observations. I mention this, Dear Reader, in the spirit of full disclosure, and as I feel it may help to situate you within the narrative and to inform your understanding and interpretation of what follows.

On a pleasantly cool Sunday, about noon, a man and woman sit across from each other at their kitchen table eating ham and cheese sandwiches. They look to be in their sixties. He is bald, moderately overweight; she is petite, birdlike, with silver hair cropped short. They are both wearing sweat suits, his maroon, hers yellow with white piping. After a long silence, she speaks.

"Peter, have you noticed something smells funny in the fridge?"

"Don't think so," he says.

"You haven't noticed an odd smell?" she says. "It's pretty strong. I'm surprised you haven't noticed."

He chews slowly, not looking up.

"Well, what do you think it might be?" she says.

"Don't know," he says. "Want me to smell it? You asking me to smell the refrigerator?"

"No," she says. "I'm just asking what you think it might be that would be giving off an odd smell. Did you put anything in there recently that would smell?"

"No idea," he says. "I'll check if you want. That make you happy?"

He begins to push himself up out of his chair.

"No," she says, placing a palm on the table. The table surface ripples out around her hand like disturbed pond water. "Don't bother."

"Okay."

He settles back in his seat and takes a sip of milk. She waits for him to finish drinking. He sets the glass down, wipes his mouth with the back of his hand. She touches her own glass with a finger, lightly.

"I just want to know what you think," she says.

"Think about what?"

"You know," she says. "Anything, really. The smell."

"I told you, Lil, I haven't smelled it," he says.

"I know," she says. "But, just the same, what do you think it might be?"

She smooths her napkin on her lap. The motion makes an audible whooshing sound, like wind across a microphone.

"Could be anything," he says. "Want me to go get rid of it?"

"No," she says. "I was just wondering if you noticed it, and what you thought it might be. That's all. There's probably a piece of fruit rotting in the crisper."

He draws a heavy breath, and with it the walls of the room suck in, bow out.

"Or maybe the leftovers from the Goose & Gander," she says. "Don't you think that might be it? When was that, last weekend? Don't you think that's maybe what it is?"

"Maybe."

"It could be something else, though," she says. "What else do you think it might be?"

"Dunno," he says.

"Sure you do," she says. "Just guess something."

"Why—what's going on?" he says. "What're you after?"

"Nothing," she says. "Nothing really."

She takes a sip of water, a bite of sandwich, chews and swallows in slow motion. He stares silently out an open window, which expands to encompass the entire wall. In the yard, sunlight slants down on a poplar tree. A red songbird sits silent on a shaded branch. In the close-mown grass beneath, another bird of matching color picks at the ground, chirping as it combs the area in search of food. The woman picks up her glass and puts it down without drinking.

"I bet that's it," she says. Then again, but louder, booming: "I bet that's it."

The man responds without moving his gaze.

"Bet that's what, hon?"

"The roast chicken carcass," she says. "From Sunday. I bet that's what the smell is. I meant to make broth. Now the bits that are left—the ones that haven't already been picked away and eaten up—must be decaying. Congealing."

He clears his throat softly, not dislodging anything so much as shuffling things around. It sounds like a big cat purring.

"I'm glad we solved that mystery," she says, her lips stretched tight across her teeth in a rictus of a smile.

She picks up her plate and glass from the table, walks to the sink to rinse her dishes.

"You know," she says. "You know what would be strange? If it were a body. A dead body. Rotting in the fridge. What if the smell I've been smelling—what if it were a human body?"

"What?" he says.

The water rushing from the tap sounds like a fire hose.

"A human body," she says again. "What if it was?"

"Why—how would it have gotten there?" he says.

"I don't know. Maybe it was someone who didn't feel like living anymore," she says. "Maybe they climbed in there. To die. Suffocated. Or starved to death."

"Would be ironic," he says. "Starving inside a box full of food."

He starts chuckling and the chuckle turns to a cackle.

"Maybe it was the cold that did them in," she says.

"I'd just as soon stop this," he says. "If it's all the same to you."
Dead silence.

"It wouldn't have started if you'd just talk to me," she says.

"Well," he says. "We're talking now, aren't we?"

She looks at the old, dust-covered analog clock, which has grown legs and is crawling, spiderlike, across the wall. 12:25.

"I'm going to fix myself a drink and sit in the other room," she says. "Will you join me?"

She pours herself a gin and tonic, mostly gin, goes into the next room and sits down in an armchair. She finishes the drink in two gulps. Then her head rolls gently sideways and detaches cleanly from her neck, making a thin, reedy snapping sound, and tumbles with a soft thud onto the floor. He remains in his seat at the table. His feet, legs, and buttocks all melt down into his socks, becoming a puddle of viscous goo. His eyes are still directed out the window, their gaze unfocused.

ROUTINE

The following is a reprint of a computer-printed document. The original was in 12-point Arial font on medium-weight white paper. It appears to be one portion of a larger clinical intake survey. I feel justified in reprinting it since there was no patient name or identifying information attached and because it was left (rather carelessly) in a public location.

I found the document neatly folded in the hip pocket of a pair of men's chinos—pressed, lightly worn, size 30/32—which were hanging out of the chute of a used clothing donation bin behind the Odsburg Public Library. For the record, I did not take the chinos, but shoved them back into the donation bin, even though they were my size and in good condition.

Odsburg Clinical Therapy Associates
Dr. Timothy Weiss, PhD

Prospective Client Questionnaire
Part 3b

In this section, please outline a typical day in your life. Be as detailed as possible.

6:00 a.m. – Wake up. Turn off alarm. Take Odslexa for sadness.

6:05 a.m. – Untangle clothes. Roll off couch. Shower, shave, get dressed.

6:30 a.m. – Breakfast. Oatmeal with raisins or fried eggs with toast. Eat leaning over kitchen sink. Take Odstolic for hypertension.

7:00 a.m. – Drive to work. Tune radio to *Wake Up, Odsburg*. Gaze wistfully at bridge abutments, loose guardrails.

7:30 a.m. – Arrive at work. Take extra-large cup of Stardust coffee for fatigue.

7:45 a.m. – Answer emails. Generate work-group status reports. Prepare presentation about upcoming product launch.

8:55 a.m. – Take Odslibrium for anxiety (prophylactic).

9:00 a.m. – Deliver presentation about upcoming product launch.

9:45 a.m. – Receive feedback from superiors necessitating total overhaul of plans for upcoming product launch.

9:55 a.m. – Take Odslonopin for anxiety (palliative).

10:00 a.m. – Take second extra-large cup of Stardust coffee for redoubled fatigue.

10:05 a.m. – Take several deep breaths to soothe heart palpitations.

10:15 a.m. – Morning break. Skim news blogs to distract from existential angst.

10:30 a.m. – Work-group status meeting. Half-listen to discussion about radically streamlined workflows in advance of upcoming product launch.

12:00 p.m. – Lunch. Burrito bowl or BLT wrap from place downstairs. Eat at workstation. Take Odseprazol for acid reflux/indigestion. Take Ods-eaze for gas/bloating. Read more news blogs.

12:45 p.m. – Brainstorming session. Per superiors' exhortations: Generate game-changing/paradigm-shattering/next-level concepts w/r/t upcoming product launch. Formulate statistically proven strategies to become premier services and products provider within targeted demographic sub-sector vis-a-vis leveraging social media to maximize ROI, etc.

2:45 p.m. – Re-revise/edit e-brochure copy for upcoming product launch.

5:00 p.m. – Leave work. Take second Odslexa for sadness. Wash down with flat, warm soda in takeout cup left in cupholder from yesterday, possibly day before. Turn on afternoon drive time radio, Heavy T and Goozer, WODS 89.3. Roll down window. Listen for ambulances. Listen for some kind of sign. Gaze wistfully at opposite sides of bridge abutments, stretches of road with no guardrails at all, broad sides of cinder block buildings set close to the two-lane highway.

5:30 p.m. – Arrive home. Drop keys, shoes inside front door.

5:45 p.m. – Dinner. Microwaved turkey loaf or Asian-inspired stir-fry from freezer. Eat standing up at kitchen counter.

6:00 p.m. – Sit down in front of television. Take two to five alcoholic drinks for general malaise. Canned beer, boxed wine, or vodka and soda.

8:45 p.m. – Take half-gram of indica/sativa/scraped-together crumbs, vaporized, for still feeling too much.

10:00 p.m. – Fall asleep on couch w/ television on.

11:30 p.m. – Wake up on couch. Consider moving to bed.

Don't bother. Take Odsopor for sleeplessness. Fall back asleep w/ television still on.

2:45 a.m. – Wake up to light/noise from television. Take second Odsopor for sleeplessness. Take double-strength, extended-release Odseprazol for persistent acid reflux. Take generous handful of assorted pills for overwhelming nighttime sadness tinged with nonspecific longing. Turn off television, fall asleep a third time.

4:45 a.m. – Wake to first sunlight through windows. Pull blanket over head. Lie very still. Clench eyes shut. Try hard not to think about morning/repetition/monotony/routine.

4:55 a.m. – Toss/turn. Take nth Odslexa for sadness. Take third Odsopor for sleeplessness. Take nth+1 Odslexa for sadness. Wish for sleep, knowing even if it comes it won't bring relief. Consider taking whole bottles of pills for sadness/sleeplessness/ defeatism/desperation. Consider merits/drawbacks of final, eternal slumber. Question concept of eternity. Contemplate possibility of afterlife/reincarnation; become sobered by smallness of man/vastness of cosmos/profundity of the unknown. Mull over futility/escape/futility of escape. Alight briefly on awareness of deep/basic/molecular-level connectedness to all other human/non-human beings; feel momentarily buoyed. Ultimately return to recognition of life's apparent/apparently inescapable meaninglessness. Decide not to decide and, for now, refrain from making any decisions that can't be taken back.

5:55 a.m. – Doze off into tense, sweaty sleep, filled with what feels like hours' worth of vivid stress dreams.

6:00 a.m. – Wake up. Turn off alarm. Take Odslexa for sadness.

CSI

Below is a copy of a copy of a Trumbull County Sheriff's Department incident report. I found the pink carbon slip snagged and dangling in some shrubbery in one of the older residential portions of town. The reporting officer appears to have been Deputy Eric Hawkins, referred to earlier, whose story you may recall.

The paper was torn and crumpled but still legible. The handwriting was something of a scrawl—it looked like a rush job. Perhaps Deputy Hawkins had to respond to another call, or maybe he just didn't want to stick around. In any case, he looked to have been in a hurry.

Trumbull County Sheriff's Office
Incident Report

Case No.: 021410
Date/Time: Aug. 10, 21:10
Reporting Officer: E. Hawkins, Deputy
Report prepared by: E. Hawkins

Detail of event: Responded to call from resident Ella Robinson, reporting presence of unidentified animal or animals in 400 block of Dutch Elm Drive. Resident reported hearing strange sounds coming from near front porch. Described as alternating howl/moan/grunt. Resident looked out windows, saw shadowy movement, said it looked like two forms, rather large, hunched, moonlit pale, smudged with gray. Possibly wolves or large-breed dogs. Resident said she did not see animal or animals clearly, was not wearing her glasses. When resident turned on porch lights, animal(s) retreated behind neighbor's hedge. Resident saw trashcans overturned, refuse strewn, what looked like a trail of dripping blood, scattered fur.

Actions taken: Conducted visual search of the area, including behind neighbor's hedge. Did not see animal(s) present. Did not hear sounds described above. Smelled foul odor, or combination of odors. Somewhat like singed hair, also roasting/rotting meat, also red wine. Collected samples of blood-type substance, fur material, and entered into evidence. Blood-type substance was dark in color, almost black, smelled sweet-pungent. Fur/hair material not so much white/gray, as resident described, but closer to sandy blond. Encouraged resident to contact if any further suspicious activity should occur.

Summary: Animal(s) causing disturbance, sighted by resident. Deputy responded. Animals not found. Cause of disturbance unconfirmed.

HUNGER PANGS

I came upon the couple, both of them probably mid-thirties, crouching beside a large, rectangular hole in the middle of a lush green lawn. The crater gaped like the raw space where a tooth had been pulled—one conspicuous gap in a jaw full of tidy historic homes. The couple was naked, sooty, and dusted with plaster, with smudges of food smeared on their faces. She was the only one to speak. While she talked, he glowered at me, slavering, like a starving man sizing up a steak.

I came home hungry and he had already started cooking. He was hungry too, he said. He made a feast: rack of lamb, whipped potatoes, braised greens. We ate it all. We ate it fast. And we washed it down with a nice pinot noir. Feeling festive and restless, and still hungry, we made a pot roast. I chopped the carrots and onions and garlic while he salted and seared the meat. When that was done and gone, we pulled cheese and grapes from the fridge, water crackers from the pantry, and a second bottle of wine, a halfway-decent sauvignon blanc. We made short work of that, then moved on to some single-barrel bourbon and Salvadoran cigars—his boss gave him the bottle and the box with his last bonus. He wondered aloud what he had been saving them for. It was only ten and we were wakeful and we were hungry and so we kept on. A half-carton of orange juice, extra pulp, passed back and forth, alternating with swigs from a gallon of sweet tea; a punch bowl full of corn flakes with two serving spoons between us. We found things we didn't know existed in corners of kitchen cabinets. Things we must have bought, but who knows when. A tub of chocolate frosting. A tin of dried sardines. A few packets of ramen, chicken flavor, reduced sodium.

Before long we were scraping bottom. Scooping baking soda from the box. I emptied the salt shaker into the back of my throat and he knocked back the last of the almond extract and he looked at me like, "Okay, what next?" Nothing was left; the shelves were empty. The kitchen was unkempt. The litter of boxes and jars left us up to our ankles in drift. So we ordered some pizzas and buffalo wings and pad kee mao and saag paneer, and when the bell rang we waded toward the door. We didn't waste time with plates or forks, we just tore open the cartons and gulped it all down.

When we'd called all the restaurant numbers we knew, when we'd finished the takeout and tossed down the boxes, we wiped at our mouths with our fists and went on. We slipped off our shoes and gnawed at the leather. Tore off our shirts and shredded the cotton, which pilled in our teeth and got stuck in our throats. Swallowed the buttons like vitamin pills. Then we took to the bathroom and bedroom and den: ripped white feathers from pillows and tan sheets from the bed, pulled out coils and batting and memory foam, digested the lampshades and lightbulbs alike. And from under the bed—where the bed had been—we grabbed the dust bunnies that hid. We squeezed out tubes of toothpaste, vials of mouthwash, and shampoo and hand soap and painkiller capsules.

When the faucets and fixtures and fittings were finished, we paused for a moment, then dug further in. We pulled up the carpet and splintered the floor. Picked our teeth and kept picking. We stripped off the paint from the walls and dissolved it in water and drank by the pitcher and still we were hungry, still we weren't full. We dug into the walls and munched hunks of plaster, slurped wires like spaghetti and ground down the pipes. Our teeth were half-wrecked and our eardrums were ringing, but neither of us had an endgame in sight. When even the blocks of the concrete foundation were dust in our stomachs, we went for the cars. We twisted off pieces of headlights and bumpers and stretched out our jaws and jammed it all in. Then we turned our sights out to the houses around us and thought of the people inside, and we looked at each other and knew without speaking that, yes, we were thinking the same.

BFF

The following is transcribed from one of my many digital audio recordings (audio file #3127, minute 49:24–58:51). It was on there when I played it back, though I don't remember recording it. I discovered it months after I had left Odsburg, while sifting through files to begin compiling this book. The speaker is unknown, though context clues suggest an adult male named Vernon.

Carl shuffled in and slumped down across from me in a booth in the far back corner of the Silver Spoon Diner. He was dressed for the office, but at eight in the morning already looked disheveled. The front of his blue oxford shirt was rumpled, rain-speckled, half-untucked. His gray, pinstriped tie hung loose, crumpled like a downed kite. Stray hairs stuck up at odd angles around his bald spot. His wire-frame glasses were slightly askew and kept sliding down the sweat-slick slope of his nose. It was clear from his jerky movements he was nervous.

"Hey, how you doing? You okay, Carl?" I said.

"Hello, Vernon. Thanks for meeting me here," he said.

"Of course. What are friends for?" I said.

"Friends—right—we are—certainly have been," he said.

"You're acting weird, Carl. Is something wrong?" I said.

"Well, the thing is—the thing is—"

His voice caught in his throat. He looked down at his hands, clenched into tight, white fists. Then he started again.

"The thing is, I'm pretty sure—that is to say, I suspect—I mean, I think—"

"Come on, Carl. Whatever it is, just say it," I said.

"Okay. I've determined, Vernon, that you're, well, that you're imaginary," he said.

"Wait. What?" I asked.

"You're not real. You're an illusion produced by my mind," he said.

"I know what 'imaginary' means," I said.

"Well then, what's the confusion?" he asked.

"How can you suggest I'm imaginary when I'm sitting here talking to you?" I said.

"Dr. Weiss told me you might ask that," he said.

"Dr. Wise?" I asked.

"My psychiatrist," he said.

"I don't believe this," I said.

"And it's Weiss, not 'Wise'—w-e-i-s-s—a soft 's,'" he said.

At that point Carl didn't say anything for a few moments. He sat there wringing his hands and staring at the fake wood grain on the tabletop. Then he swallowed hard, like a skinny snake with a fat hamster in his throat.

He said:

"Look, Vernon, there's something more—and please don't interrupt. This is hard for me. You need to understand. But I think it would be best if you would stop appearing. It's unhealthy—to keep talking to you like this. I'm thirty-eight, for Chrissakes. It's—it's—maladaptive."

And I said:

"Maladaptive. You know what that sounds like? A fancy doctor word—a word you wouldn't have used before. Like you're just regurgitating what Dr. Weiss-sssss tells you. Do you know what that word means, Carl—'regurgitating'? It means throwing up! Vomiting! Spitting out undigested! As in, 'You're making me so sick I'm about to regurgitate all over the table.'"

I was off on a bit of a rant, I admit. But then I saw the look on Carl's face—so pitiful, so forlorn. His eyes turned glossy behind his glasses. And I realized he didn't *want* to do this: the doctor had put him up to it. So I tried a different approach.

I said:

"Let's hold on a minute, not lose our heads prematurely, okay? Think about it: we've been through so much together, Carl, you and me. In and out of trouble together so many times—since we were kids! The time you drew on the walls and blamed it on me, but your mom didn't buy it. And in third grade, when you threw cottage cheese at Ricky Noonan? You got sent to the principal's office, and I sat with you all afternoon! And in high school, when we rode a shopping cart into the lake. You nearly drowned, you could have died! Who dragged you out and kept you conscious 'til the paramedics arrived? Oh, and the trip to Ape Cave! When we were befriended-slash-attacked by a family of bats. Or the rough patch I helped you through, when Amy broke up with you. And we TP'ed her yard and dropped dog turds on her porch. And she threatened a restraining order. And we went for a consolatory comfort food binge at the Golden Corral! Or the time you were accused of embezzling from the credit union. I stayed home with you to watch game shows and eat Cheetos all day. Those whole two months while you were on administrative leave! Until your name was finally cleared and you were allowed to return to work! You don't think I had other things to do? Other places to be? But I was there for you, Carl, and I never regretted a minute of it. I could go on for hours—there are just so many memories!"

He said:

"Yeah, we've had some times—been through a lot together, that's for sure."

Remembering all that, Carl smiled. Then he was smiling and crying at the same time. And then my eyes started welling up, too. Right about then a waitress came around to the table. A young woman whose nametag said "Agnes." Seeing her coming, Carl wiped the tears off his face with a napkin.

"Can I get you anything?" asked Agnes.

"Yes. Two tall coffees. One for me, and one for my imaginary friend," said Carl.

Let me tell you: the look Agnes gave Carl, when he said "one for my imaginary friend." She looked so skeptical, so hesitant—afraid, even—like she thought Carl was crazy. Like she didn't believe for a second that I was imaginary. Like she could see me there, plain as day, and knew I was 100 percent real. That look was very reassuring. I could have hugged Agnes for that.

I didn't. But I could have.

"Um, sure, okay," she said.

Then she walked away, quickly. When she came back a minute later, she set two coffees on the table, side by side. Then she speed-walked away again. After Agnes left, Carl turned back to me. He looked me straight in the eye this time.

He said:

"Look, Vernon, you've been there for me through thick and thin. And I appreciate it, I really do, but the thing is— There's no denying—no getting around the fact—You're an aberration, a mental projection, and it's not healthy—"

I said:

"Jesus, again with the psychobabble. Don't listen to that doctor, listen to how you feel."

For a moment, he looked conflicted. He tugged his left earlobe and frowned.

"No offense ... I feel I'd like to be a normal guy with normal real-person friends," he said.

"No offense?" I said.

Carl looked around the café like he was suddenly worried what people might think. As for me, I was definitely taking offense. He could claim all day that I'm imaginary, but the pain, the heartbreak, the betrayal—the hurt I felt in that moment? It was real. Of course, I didn't want Carl to know how much he'd wounded me. So I went with anger instead.

"Screw you, Carl. Screw you!" I said.

"Keep it down, Vernon, you're making a scene. People are starting to stare," he said.

"What do I care? I'm not real, remember? How can I care what anybody thinks?" I said.

"Just calm down, Vernon. Please just calm down," he said.

He made a "calming" gesture with his hands. It looked like he was pressing down on something invisible in front of him. Trying to stuff it under the table. He looked around again. People were definitely staring. Suddenly, I had an idea. I leaned across the table and lowered my voice to a whisper.

"Carl, how do you know Dr. Weiss is real?" I said.

"Well," he said.

"Well?" I said.

"I guess maybe I don't know for sure," he said.

"So why let a maybe-maladaptive-figment-doctor turn you against your best friend?" I said.

"But I did see his medical license and diploma," he said.

"So?" I said.

"And he spoke to his secretary, so either they're both imaginary ..." he said.

"Which is possible," I said.

"Or, they're both real," he said.

He squinted and looked me hard in the face for a moment. Something about that look, I didn't like it.

"Now I think about it, Vern, I've never seen anyone else talk to you," he said.

"I'm just an introvert. People can sense that," I said.

"And look, you're not even drinking your coffee! I bet you can't," he said.

"Sure I can. I just have a long drive and don't want to have to pee," I said.

"Oh yeah? What kind of car do you drive?" he said.

I hesitated, trying to come up with the name of a real car that real people drive. It's funny, the little details that make all the difference in the world. The difference, for example, between keeping and losing your best and only friend. I kicked myself for not noticing any of the names on the cars in the parking lot outside. Finally, I decided to take a guess; too much hesitation, and I'd have lost him anyway. I said I drove a Ford Tuberous—I thought it sounded plausible. Carl's eyes flashed. He looked triumphant.

"There's no such thing!" he said.

"Fine! I guess you got me, then," I said.

"I guess I did," he said.

Then, after a couple seconds, his face fell. He sucked in a deep breath and blew it out with a sigh. His shoulders slumped and he leaned back into his chair. His exuberance was replaced by a kind of sad-but-satisfied resolve. And that's when I knew it was really over. So I gave him a little parting speech—a speech that I think was pretty good, especially considering it was totally off-the-cuff, without notes or anything.

I said:

"You don't want me around anymore, that's fine. I'll find someone else to spend my time with, because you know what, Carl? You suck! You suck suck suck suck suck! I guess I'll go hang out with the Tooth Fairy. Or the Loch Ness Monster.

Or some other people you don't believe are real. How about that? I'll throw a party and invite everybody: Gnomes! Bigfoots! Martians! Anyway, there's no use hanging around here. Because if there's one thing I've learned, it's to not stick around where I'm not wanted. And one more thing, Carl: it's your loss!"

Then I got up from my seat and walked to the door of the diner. I left the coffee sitting there on the table to show Carl I didn't want his charity. And I waited, stubbornly, with my back to Carl, until a pretty young woman opened the door. Then I ducked underneath her arm and slipped out silently into the drab, drizzly morning. As I walked away, I glanced back just once to see Carl still sitting there, alone at a table for two, with two cups of coffee getting cold.

CODA

As I mentioned at the beginning of this book, my goal is the preservation and the elevation of what one might be tempted to call "small" stories—the personal anecdote, the local legend, the otherwise-overlooked atom of accidental lyrical ephemera. What I hope to have achieved, if you will indulge a mixed and imperfect metaphor, is to have gathered minor notes into major chords, to have performed a kind of aggregational alchemy, uplifting the leaden scraps and castings of our human lives to the gilded status of historical artifact.

At risk of sounding self-important (or species-important), I wish to remind us that the flimsiest, most inconsequential trappings of humanity—personal anecdotes, bits of scribbled notecard, schoolroom juvenilia, etc.—are worth preserving, for ourselves and for generations to come.

We are the storytelling species. We have a profound and basic need for narrative: to be fulfilled, we must tell our stories and feel that others have heard them. And to be truly whole, we must also hear and absorb the stories of others. If we pay attention to those stories, in whatever form they might manifest, in whatever package they may be delivered to us—if we record them faithfully and listen closely—they will speak to us in the most profound ways, and we will learn from them invaluable lessons.

And so, if I have just one wish for you, Dear Reader, it is this:

that you will allow this book to open your eyes, your ears, your mind—indeed, your heart—to the myriad stories in multifold forms of those people around you. Those you know well and those you merely brush against in passing. Because it is my belief that through the sharing of stories we may become better connected, kinder, more empathetic, both as individuals and as a society. That through sharing stories, we may elevate one another in our shared humanity.

DISCLAIMER

It is the author's belief that he has the legal, ethical, and, at the very least, cosmic right to use all of the material presented in this book. Every person who was recorded either gave their express consent or was speaking in public, or quasi-public, and thereby placed their business in the hands of whomever might have been passing by. The author further states that he acquired all artifacts and cataloged items fairly, that he obtained them from public sources or in public places, discarded or on the street, or, failing that, in rooms with open or unlocked doors. Anyone taking issue with the rights of the author is encouraged to do some deep soul searching and consider whether he or she really has a legitimate issue with the subject matter at hand, and whether there might be a better use of his or her time and money than to take up a legal complaint against the author or his publisher, since legal proceedings are known to be expensive, emotionally arduous, and rarely satisfying for anyone involved.

ABOUT THE SOCIO-ANTHROPO-LINGUI-LORE-OLOGIST

Wallace Jenkins-Ross is a self-taught (and self-described) socio-anthropo-lingui-lore-ologist. His research and writing concentrate on the contemporary customs, mythologies, and artifacts of various human populations, with a focus on Anglophone North American societies. Prior to living in Odsburg, Mr. Jenkins-Ross spent time immersed in the cultures and subcultures of small towns and cities in New Mexico, New York, and New England, among other places.

When he is not in the field gathering material, Mr. Jenkins-Ross calls Northern California home. He shares custody of two purebred Alsatian dogs—Aristotle and Levi-Strauss—with his ex-wife Carolyn. In spare moments, he has lately been learning the mountain dulcimer, as well as brewing his own kombucha, which has developed a small following at the farmers markets in Arcata and Eureka.

This is his first successfully published book.

Matt Tompkins is the author of *Failures* (Monday Night Press), *Souvenirs and Other Stories* (Conium Press), and *Topia* (Red Bird Chapbooks). His stories have appeared in the *New Haven Review*, *Post Road*, and online at the *Carolina Quarterly*, *Fiction Southeast*, and *Puerto del Sol*. He works as a copy editor and lives in Virginia with his wife and daughter.

ACKNOWLEDGMENTS

First and foremost, I want to thank my wife, Kori, whose support and encouragement have been indispensable, and who shows me, again and again, that anything worth doing requires persistence and hard work.

Also my daughter, Greta, whose existence is inspiration, and whose boundless imagination reminds me every day of the magical, transportive power of stories.

Big thanks, too, to Jake Goldman, who is a good friend for having read countless drafts of countless stories, some that appear here and plenty of others that were only ever destined for the drawer.

And I would like to acknowledge, in alphabetical order, all the literary magazines, journals and small presses that published individual pieces from Odsburg in earlier forms: *Apt*, *Atticus Review*, *Avis*, *Blue Mesa Review*, *Cheap Pop*, Conium Press, *Cooper Street*, *CutBank*, *Fiction Southeast*, *Firewords*, *H_ngm_n*, *Little Patuxent Review*, *Monday Night* and Monday Night Press, *New Haven Review*, *Ostrich Review*, *Penny*, *Post Road*, *Puerto del Sol*, *Quail Bell*, Red Bird Chapbooks, tNY Press, and *Transverse Journal*. Thanks, as well, to the many places that declined these stories, for being a necessary part of the process.

I want to thank everyone at Ooligan Press who worked with me on Odsburg, especially acquisitions editors Alyssa

Schaffer and Joanna Szabo, who saw a glimmer of promise in the book in its partially formed state and took a chance on it and on me; the editorial team, particularly Managing Editor Madison Schultz, who ushered the manuscript through multiple rounds of revisions; the design team, who brought the artifacts of Odsburg visually to life; and Project Manager Marina Garcia, who seamlessly spliced all the threads.

And finally, I would like to thank you, Dear Reader, for picking up this book and devoting a little bit of your precious time to it. Thanks for visiting Odsburg. I hope you enjoyed your stay, and I hope you'll come back again sometime.

PREVIOUS PUBLICATIONS

"Hunger Pangs" *CutBank*, 2019

"Alpha, Beta, Delta, Theta" *Monday Night*, 2017 Issue 16

"TOMWABFAM" *Puerto del Sol*, October 2017

"Hypothetical" *Sixpenny*, 2016

"Seeking Advice and/or Assistance re: Mountain Lions" *Fiction Advocate*, 2016

"Visceral" *Fiction Southeast*, 2016

"Seeking Advice and/or Assistance re: Mountain Lions" *Post Road*, 2016 Issue 29

"Aeolus" *Avis* #2, October 2016

"Spinning Jinnies" *Blue Mesa Review*, December 2016, Issue 34

"Deep-six" *CHEAP POP*, 2015

"Mel and the Microphones" *Atticus Review*, 2015

"Please Please Please Please Please Keep Smiling" *Monday Night*, 2015

"Souvenirs" *Transverse*, 2015

"The Water Cycle" *New Haven Review*, 2015 Issue 16

"The World on Fire" *Little Patuxent Review*, 2015 Issue 18

"BFF" *Firewords Quarterly*, Fall 2015 Issue 5

"Regarding Your Modeling Portfolio" *Ostrich Review*, 2015 Issue 7

"A Man Walks into a Bar" *Apt*, September 2014

"Late Breakfast at the Corvair" *Quail Bell*, 2012

"Eulogy" *H_NGM_N*, 2015 Issue 17

"In the Space Below, Please Provide an Example of Your Typical Daily Schedule" *EEEL*, 2014

"The Dog after the Rabbit ..." *Cooper Street*, 2014 Issue 1

OOLIGAN PRESS

Ooligan Press is a student-run publishing house rooted in the rich literary culture of the Pacific Northwest. Founded in 2001 as part of Portland State University's Department of English, Ooligan is dedicated to the art and craft of publishing. Students pursuing master's degrees in book publishing staff the press in an apprenticeship program under the guidance of a core faculty of publishing professionals.

Project Managers
Marina Garcia
Ivy Knight

Acquisitions
Ari Mathae
Taylor Thompson

Design
Jenny Kimura
Denise
   Morales Soto

Marketing
Sydney Kiest
Sydnee Chelsey

Digital
Kate Barnes

Social Media
Sadie Verville

Editing
Madison Schultz
Emma Hovley

Book Production
Erin Bass
Sanjay Dharawat
Alyssa Flynn
Esa Grigsby
Jennifer Guiher
Monica Hay
Des Hewson
Tia Hilts
Elise Hitchings
Megan Huddleston
Chris Leal
Hilary Louth
Kristen Ludwigsen
Faith Muñoz
Meagan Nolan
Nicole O'Connor
Victoria Raible

Joanna Szabo
Monique Vieu
Allyson Yenerall
Hanna Ziegler